"Like one of Jesus' parables, *Exit 36* avoids moral lessons or easy answers. Instead, Robert Farrar Capon explores suicide, adultery, and the general failures that beset both the characters in this novel and all of us with them. And he does it without moral outrage or shoulder-shrugging apathy. Instead, Capon looks directly at the agony of a fallen world through the mystery of the reconciliation of everything and everybody in Christ. Whatever scandals one might find in this book, however, the scandal of grace through the death and resurrection of Jesus triumphs over it all. Capon's voice is needed now as much as it ever has been."

— The Very Rev. Mark Strobel
Dean, Gethsemane Cathedral, Fargo

Also by Robert Farrar Capon:

Bed & Board: Plain Talk About Marriage (2018)

The Man Who Met God in a Bar:
The Gospel According to Marvin: A Novel (2017)

More Theology & Less Heavy Cream:
The Domestic Life of Pietro & Madeleine (2016)

Light Theology & Heavy Cream:
The Culinary Adventures of Pietro & Madeleine (2004)

Genesis, The Movie (2003)

Kingdom, Grace, Judgment:
Paradox, Outrage, and Vindication in the Parables of Jesus (2002)

The Fingerprints of God:
Tracking the Divine Suspect Through a History of Images (2000)

The Foolishness of Preaching:
Proclaiming the Gospel Against the Wisdom of the World (1997)

Between Noon and Three:
Romance, Law, and the Outrage of Grace (1997)

The Astonished Heart:
Reclaiming the Good News from
the Lost-and-Found of Church History (1996)

The Romance of the Word:
One Man's Love Affair with Theology (1995)

Health, Money, and Love . . .
And Why We Don't Enjoy Them (1994)

The Mystery of Christ . . .
And Why We Don't Get It (1993)

Capon on Cooking (1983)

A Second Day: Reflections on Remarriage (1980)

Party Spirit: Some Entertaining Principles (1979)

Food for Thought: Resurrecting the Art of Eating (1978)

The Supper of the Lamb: A Culinary Reflection (1969)

AND COMING SOON FROM MOCKINGBIRD
The Youngest Day

EXIT 36
A FICTIONAL CHRONICLE

BY

ROBERT FARRAR CAPON

A MOCKINGBIRD
PUBLICATION

Copyright © 2018 Valerie Capon

All rights reserved.
No part of this book may be used or reproduced in any manner whatsoever without written permission, except in the case of brief quotations embodied in critical articles or reviews.

Excerpt from "Horae Canonicae" by W. H. Auden, reprinted from *Collected Shorter Poems 1927-1957*, originally printed with permission of Random House, Inc. Copyright © 1955 by W. H. Auden.

Cover art by Maddy Green; design by Tom Martin.
Published 2018 by Mockingbird Ministries.

ISBN-13: 978-0-9989171-7-7
ISBN-10: 0-9989171-7-6

Mockingbird Ministries ("Mockingbird") is an independent not-for-profit ministry seeking to connect, comment upon and explore the Christian faith with and through contemporary culture. Mockingbird disclaims any affiliation, sponsorship, or connection with any other entity using the words "Mockingbird" and "Ministries" alone or in combination.

Robert told me that this book came to be because of the death of a fellow priest. He wanted to try his hand at writing dialogue, and so he fictionalized the events leading up to and after his friend's death. He had no idea that the story would lead him into the mysterious workings of the Holy Spirit. He also preached on the Scriptures that dealt with eternal life and answered questions posed by his parishioners at the coffee hours after church. This opened the door for more conversations in the books that followed.

Valerie Capon
Shelter Island, NY, 2017

FOREWORD

By Chad Bird

In the early days of December, I crawl up into my attic, step over a couple of rafters, and take a deep breath to blow a year's worth of dust off a long cardboard box. On the side, written in faded black marker, is the name, Barbara. Then down we go, man and box, back over the rafters, back down the ladder, and into the family room, where the annual ritual begins. Cut the tape, open the box, and piece by piece, begin to remove and organize the contents. A wobbly, three-legged stand. A green, six-foot pole. And a pile of prickly, plastic limbs that look like the ugly cousin of mother nature's evergreen beauty. After an hour or so of disentangling and reassembling—and probably a drink or three—the conical tree stands tall and proud, ready to have its green plainness festooned with the winking colors of Christmas cheer.

But this is no ordinary tree. It has a stubborn streak.

Weave a hundred strands of bright lights through its greenery, let a thousand happy ornaments swing and sing from its limbs, and the tree itself will stand there like a tight-lipped choir girl who won't join in "Joy to the World." It's Barbara's tree—a gift she gave my family shortly before she drove to south Texas, shut off the engine in a city park, and swallowed the darkness inside her by swallowing a bottleful of pills. And now her tree stands there, our family's visual memory of her and the friendship we shared. And try as we might to make her tree as beautiful, sparkling, and happy as we can, it's hard not to see those branches decorated and dripping with tears.

I think this December, and maybe every December after that, I'll try something new. I'll pull a chair up in front of Barbara's tree, open *Exit 36*, and begin to read Robert Capon's words aloud. The whole story, beginning to end. Let them wash over the room, the tree, me, the memories, the regrets, the unanswered and unresolvable questions. Then, when I'm finished, I'll close the book and prop it up against the base of the tree. Because if there's a story this tree needs to hear, my family needs to hear, and all who have lost Barbaras of their own need to hear, it's the one you now hold in your hands.

Robert Capon does in this book what he always does with unparalleled skill: he stirs the ultimate questions of life into the seemingly un-ultimate, daily grind of characters' lives who make a royal mess of their relationships, friendships, and vocations. A priest who's so done with life he ends it all by driving his car into a concrete embankment at 80 mph. Another priest—the narrator—who, when he isn't trying to get to the bottom of the reasons for his colleague's suicide, comforting the widow, or producing a brilliant theology about the reconciliation of all things in Christ, is playing with the fire of attraction to the dead man's lovely mistress. Sprinkle in some brief but lively excurses about the nastiness of church politics, food and drinks, and life on the east coast, and you have the priceless gem called Exit 36. So is this a novel or a theological work, a narrative or a sermon? Yes, and more. Put suicide, ministry, adultery, eschatology, gospel, Jesus, and curvy mistresses all onto the literary table, pour some wine, settle into your seat, and gaze in wonder at the feast that only Capon could prepare with such brilliance, wit, and profundity.

Capon is one of those rare birds among Christian authors. He actually takes seriously the fact that, when God was deliberating how best to unveil the profoundest mysteries of the world, he jettisoned philosophical treatises, systematic theologies, and Q & A catechisms. He chose instead to sit us children down on the front porch, light his pipe, and say, "Kids, let me tell you a story." A story full of naked people and talking snakes, polygamous kings and street-smart prostitutes, giants and blind men and prophets smelling like they crawled out of a fish. When God wants us to know something, to really know something, to stake our very lives on the truth of it: he tells us a story. He punctuates the narrative with prayers and psalms, proverbs and sermons, scolding letters and hair-raising apocalypses, but these only serve to spice things up a bit. And as we hear the story, we are swallowed up by it, sting at its pains and laugh at its jokes, and—strangest of all—realize the story we are hearing about others turns out to be the story of ourselves.

In this way, Exit 36 falls smack dab in the middle of the biblical genre. More than the story of one month in the life of a parish priest who's juggling counseling, preaching, flirting, drinking, and exploring his own mortality, it's the story of the God standing behind the veil of the story. The God who isn't bound by the tick-tocking, chronological flow of our lives from diapers to dentures. The God for whom the future is not "out there" or the past "back there," but for whom everything that ever has been, is, or will be, is simply, his very own Today. And that Today, that God-Day, is the day that enfolds all of our days, that sucks them into its vortex and transforms them into what it is. More importantly, that Today is the day of salvation, of the reconciliation of everyman and everything in the crucified and resurrected Christ, who holds the whole kit and caboodle inside his own skin.

The suicide? Reconciled. The widow? Reconciled. The mistress, the gossipers, the gravedigger, the children, and the storytelling priest? All reconciled. Not one after the other. Not when they zipped up and quit frequenting cheap hotel rooms. Not when they confessed and toed the line. Not in that millisecond of righteous regret before the vehicle slammed into the concrete. Not in yesterday's repentance or tomorrow's amendment of life. But all in that grand and all-compassing Today of the Lamb slain from the foundation of the world. They all fit into his scars. What's more, they've all been there from the get-go, from the pre-Genesis days, before creation, before the fall, before the last curtain call when trumpets blast and glorified bodies start popping out of graveyards like champagne corks. Above all those historical moments stands the Lamb, holding together all humanity in the reconciliation that's handcuffed to no clock or calendar, but free in the never-beginning and never-ending Today of salvation.

This December, when I pull up a chair in front of Barbara's tree, and read this book aloud, those are the thoughts that'll be frolicking inside my head. What really matters is not her divorce, her depression, her closetful of skeletons or her heart empty of hope—what matters are not those dark and fragmented moments of her day-to-day existence, but the God of love who wrapped her in his arms before she even arrived in this broken life.

Capon ushers us into the story where Barbara and me, you and the priests, and this whole wide world of jacked up, navel-gazing, time-bound and sin-worn creatures are already included in Today's party where the Lamb pours and refills drinks for us all, where the Father is tickled pink with us, and where life in abundance is all there is to be found.

PREFACE

THIS BOOK MAKES use of a device which, if it is not to everyone's liking, still has served me well enough to make me think it an acceptable way of writing theology at the present time. Indeed, by now it may be more second nature to me than device. I refer, of course, to my penchant for writing with both hands—for dealing with two subjects at once. In the present case, the left, or theologizing, hand draws the themes of eschatology: Death, Judgment, Hell and Heaven. The right hand—which in *Bed and Board* wrote about family life, in *The Supper of the Lamb* about cooking and in *Uncles, Peacock,* and *Fox* about clowning in the classroom—draws here a somewhat straighter subject: the chronicling of one month in the life of a parish priest.

The chronicle, for obvious reasons, is entirely fictitious. In large part, it deals with communications which, if known to be matters of fact, would clearly be privileged. Accordingly, none of the characters is based on any specific person, living or dead. Any resemblances to actual people are coincidental and unintended.

The setting is mid-Suffolk County, Long Island in May of 1973, with two fictional alterations: There is no Episcopal Church in Coram; those familiar with the area will realize that the Parish of St. Aidan which I have supplied is more of a good thing than could ever come out of the Coram they know. Likewise, the fictitious Parish of Grace Church, Port Jefferson tends to be portrayed in a warmer light than the Episcopal Church's somewhat less than feverish recent past in that village actually warrants.

While the right hand thus logs the comings and goings of priest and people, however, the left hand is busy at the other end of the cutting board, peeling away at the great eschatological onion with which, the Faith tells us, God flavors to perfection the final all-satisfying stew. It begins its work, naturally enough, with the outer and largest part of the onion, with the most certain and considerable of the Four Last Things, with Death. But then, itself reeking of its subject, it peels on toward the center of the Mystery, finding its matter ever smaller as it nears the heart, knowing less about Judgment than about death, less about Hell than about Judgment and least of all about the bright, small whiteness which is all it has of Heaven—until finally, at the last, deepest core, it finds the green fuse, the thrust which was what the whole was all about, the Christ dead and risen, by whom the being of everyman and everything is reconciled and raised.

Admittedly, peeling onions is tearful, smelly work, and the prospect of so large a specimen tends to put us off. There is a curse of raw onion which only slow simmering can cure. But the dish is worth the wait, and God meanwhile draws us home by the very nose he first offended. Trudging down the back streets of our years toward the youngest day, we catch in the wind the scent of what he's cooking and the spring comes back into our step. Life is not just a bad lunch followed by no supper and a lonely bed. It smells like a very good dinner after all—something with fried onions in it. And who knows? Maybe later…

Robert Farrar Capon
Port Jefferson, Long Island, New York
July 1974

I

Thursday, April 26th

JACOBS—REV. THEODORE, ON *April 25, 1973, Rector of St. Aidan's Church (Episcopal), Coram, L.I., N.Y. Beloved husband of Anne, loving son of Bertha, loving father of David and Rebekah, devoted brother of Joan and Charles. Service at St. Aidan's Church on Friday, April 27, at 11:00 A.M. Interment private. In lieu of flowers, contributions to St. Aidan's Memorial Fund, P.O. Box 4117, Coram, N.Y., will be appreciated.*

II

Tuesday, May 8th

SHE CALLED AT five, right in the middle of grace before supper.

The dash from the dining table to the office phone is a good twenty yards. The kids drop into their seats and do a countdown on the rings. One. Two. Slight pause to refresh the pre-dinner drink before heading down a hallway mined with vacuum-cleaner parts. Three. (Known as the miraculous ring, after which half the people who call me at dinnertime apparently find their problems solved and hang up.) Four. The phone, logically enough in a house with teenagers, is not on the desk but on the floor. Five. Getting the phone up off the floor while answering it means putting down the drink. Six. My Scotch slides off a stack of papers and pours itself into the open desk drawer, a drink-offering to Ma Bell.

"Hello."

"Is this Father Jansson?"

"Yes, it is."

"Father, you don't know me, but I know you. I saw you a week ago Friday at Ted Jacob's funeral. I know you must be very busy, but I wonder if it would be possible to make an appointment to see you?"

"Other things being equal, sure. Let me find my date book in this mess. What's your name?"

"Patricia Donahue."

"Where from?"

"Coram."

"Listen, can you hold on a minute? My calendar is probably in my coat pocket. I'll be right back."

Out into the hallway again. Funny how certain female voices arouse my interest. If a male stranger wants an appointment, I set it up mostly just out of duty. But push the mystery voice up an octave and make it sound thirtyish, and doing business becomes a pleasure. By the time I get back to the phone, the spilled Scotch is unlamented and the teenage nuisances are all but absolved.

"Hi. What time of day is good for you, afternoon or evening?"

"Afternoon would be better, it it's all right with you."

"How about Thursday afternoon?"

"That's fine. Could it be early, though? I have to be home by three, unless I get a sitter, or have my neighbor watch for the children."

"Let's say one, then. That too early?"

"No, it's just fine. Thank you. I hope it's not too much trouble."

We talked for a minute or so more. I took her phone number in case I had to cancel, gave her directions, and then fished a little for some hint of why she wanted to see me. Hearing none, I didn't press. All I got was the fact that she had been a member of Ted's parish. I hung up, got the ice cubes out of the envelope compartment and mopped out the drawer with Kleenex.

The voice. I remember thinking she sounded good-looking. And also reminding myself that was a lot of nonsense. And then not believing the reminder. The inverted whammy. You tell yourself she's probably grotesque; but since you do it chiefly in the hope that thinking such a thing will somehow talk the universe out of its perverse desire to foist it on you, the hope wins out and she takes up residence in your head as a knockout. I remember too, though, automatically rating her as not having had much education beyond high school.

That's another aural snap judgment. She had what I would call a moderately severe case of Long Island accent: basic Newyorkese, but pitched higher, with a nasal, whining edge. At its worst it can make the word "Father" grate on the ear like a saber-saw hitting a piece of thin plywood. College seldom cures it, but I guess I unconsciously assume it would. Hers wasn't whiningly nasal, but when she said "beautiful," it came out as "beautyful," and the "t" was voiced as if it were a "d." I reminded myself that proved nothing either. But prejudices about speech patterns are invincible, so, after two minutes' worth of conversation, I was set for Thursday at one o'clock with a dumb blonde.

III

Thursday, May 10th

She was on time. And, for once, the whammy worked. As a matter of fact, she was even better-looking than I expected, although, as usual, the expectations were miles off the target. She was about 5 feet 3 inches, 110 pounds, give or take a few, and brunette. She seemed to be about thirty-five, but she had the kind of slightly hard good looks that could throw you off five years in either direction. Firm figure, long hair, good skin. High cheekbones, a nice angular jaw and eyes that were either deep-set or tired, I couldn't tell which. Something discrepant about her as a whole, though. As if there were a distance between her looks and herself. The fitted black slacks, the yellow sweater, the costume jewelry, the practiced makeup job just this side of being overdone—all that was full of assurance. Not the kind you see coming out of Bonwit's or Bergdorf, of course.

More like very good Spiegel Catalogue, but definitely all together. It was her face that was wrong. It wasn't in on the act. It didn't so much clash with the outfit as disregard it. And ask you to disregard it. The way a nun's face sometimes seems to invite you to ignore the black habit and concentrate on her eyes. Except that the effect here was reversed. The brightness was all in the costume; the invitation was to look away from light.

Small talk from the front door to the office. Did she have any trouble finding the place? No, the directions were fine. Why didn't she sit on the couch and be comfortable? Did I mind if she smoked? Not at all. If I could find my cigar, I'd relight it.

Winstons and gold lighter out of the shoulder bag. Cigarette tamped on the side of the lighter. Lit, inhaled. Right hand cocked back, palm up. Smoke breathed out. All practiced, all together. But again, all somehow irrelevant.

"Now that I'm here I don't know where to begin."

"Start in the middle and work either way. If it's all one piece, you'll eventually cover it. How'd you come to call me up?"

"One of my girl friends knows you. Or at least she came and talked to you a couple of years ago. Her name is Sue D'Amato. She was having marriage problems at the time, and she said you helped keep her from falling apart. When all this happened, I kind of put calling you in the back of my mind, but I didn't do anything about it till Tuesday. I guess I just used up my other ideas of what to do and you were the only idea left. It's probably silly. I'm wasting your time."

"No you're not. That's what time is for. And anyway, I don't consider this a waste."

(One small flag up. False note. Good-looking women must hate the way their looks get more attention than what they're trying to say.)

"Sue D'Amato… From Middle Island, right? Married to a detective. She came to see me about four times. Did that ever break up?"

"They're still together, but mostly because she puts up with a lot more than most women would."

"That's the way it is. Makes you wonder if it's any favor to help them talk themselves out of splitting. Are you and I on the subject of marriage here?"

"Not exactly. I'm separated, and I guess you could call that part of the problem. But it's not the part that bothers me right now. That's something I more or less got used to. Well, not used to, really. It's just that when someone hurts you long enough you sort of hide inside yourself and stop loving. Then the hurt doesn't reach you as much. You can last a long time that way. I didn't leave my husband. He left me."

"What are we on then? Some hurt for which hiding doesn't work?"

"Yes. You remember when I called you, I mentioned that I saw you at Ted Jacobs's funeral? Well, I was close to him. Very close."

"For a long time?"

(A dumb question, but what else do you say when the other shoe about to drop turns out to be a boot?)

"Four years. Look, you don't have to say anything about this, do you? I mean, can it end right here? I made a promise I wouldn't say anything, but I just can't keep it."

"Go ahead and say what you need to. It won't go any further. Under the Seal."

"Well, I'm really not making a confession—at least not of what you'd usually think."

"Makes no difference, any more than what I'd usually think does."

"All right. It began six years ago when we moved to Coram. My husband is Roman Catholic, but he doesn't go to church. I was confirmed in the Episcopal Church in Mineola. For the first four years after we were married, I didn't go to church either, but then, what with wanting my children to go to Sunday school and all, I started taking them and going to church by myself.

"Long before we got to Coram, though, things had gotten pretty bad between my husband and me. He either ignored me completely or leaned all over me. He was always saying how dumb I was in front of other people. You know, 'Pat's always getting lost. Pat couldn't keep her checkbook straight if you paid her. Pat can never find her wallet.' It all sounds sort of harmless, I guess, but when it just never lets up, it eats at you. That and the jealousy.

"He was one of those men who can't let a woman see their emotions—at least not any gentle, loving ones. He liked sex well enough, but he never gave any real love. I suppose the jealousy was his way of telling me he cared, but what good is that? We'd go to a party and maybe one of the fellows would make a fuss over me. Just for enjoying myself dancing and talking, I would get two days' worth of sulking followed by hours and hours of questions and accusations. Especially if I made the mistake of letting him see I felt lovable after a party. Then when the sulks were over, he'd carry on about how I acted like a tramp and was only good for one-night stands. I don't know which was worse, waiting for the anger to hit or being hit by it. Either way, it was endless."

Cigarettes and lighter out again. Fast light this time: no tamping. She started speaking in the middle of exhaling.

"Anyway, as I said, I got so I pulled inside myself as much as I could. I suppose it was wrong, but I deliberately hoped I would stop loving him, and by and by, I did. For a while there I had this girl friend who had a nothing marriage too. We would use each other for an excuse for an evening and get dressed up and go out to a cocktail lounge. That was before singles' bars. We'd take all the attention we could get, and then leave together. It made some of the men pretty mad, and maybe it was kind of mean—a way of getting even with men—but it was fun, and they enjoyed what they got even if they didn't get everything they wanted.

"Well, naturally, my husband eventually caught on, and the roof fell in. By then, though, I was fed up with the bar scene anyhow—all the stupid arrangements, leaving one car in the Westbury railroad station, and so forth, and all the passes and the boring talk. So I did the easiest thing and handed him the phony repentance he wanted. And then I hid a little further inside myself. Look, I'm not boring you, am I? I wasn't going to talk about my marriage like this. It just seems to be the way to do it."

"No. At least you're started. Keep going."

"The surprising thing is that things actually got a little better. He had his big victory, so he was actually nice to me in public sometimes. He even seemed to want to be tender once in a while. But by then I was out of reach for anything, love or hate. Still, though, it was relatively peaceful, and I found sometimes I actually liked it. He was very good with his hands—he had a whole cellarfull of power tools. There were times at night when he'd be down there working on a piece of furniture with his lathe or something running, and I'd be upstairs reading, and I would think that maybe it would be all right—that maybe love was just for kids anyway, and I should be glad I was over it. Does that make any sense?"

"It does to me. We've been sold a bill of goods which says that falling in love is the answer to every problem. But the way we go about it, it can turn out to be the biggest problem of all. Falling out of love can be a relief."

"Well, I just thought I was strange or something. But I actually did begin to feel stronger inside. More able to rely on myself. I read a lot, I started to pray again, and best of all, I got in the habit of every now and then driving out this way to Sunken Meadow and walking on the beach. Sometimes it was so beautiful it almost hurt, and I guess I knew deep down that I wasn't really over love at all. But most of the time, it was just nice. The weather on different days. The different lights. All the things you could pick up like shells and stones and driftwood. I even tried to write some poems. They weren't much, but I liked writing them.

"Anyway, the result was that when my husband got the idea of moving, I wasn't as against it as I would have expected. Which is how I met Ted.

"By the time we moved, I had already been going to church again for two years. Not every Sunday. I felt close to God everywhere, so when I missed, I didn't feel guilty or anything. But I did go more than half the time. So, as soon as we were settled, I just went to his church the same way. It was a pretty large congregation. For a while, I just came and went and didn't get involved. He was a good preacher. He was very liberal in his politics, though, and that put me off a little at first. I suppose I was conservative like my husband. At least, politics were one problem we didn't have. He loved to sound off, and I really never thought about it, so I guess I just unconsciously followed his lead.

"After a while, though, some of Ted's ideas seemed to make sense, and if I ever did think something through, I usually ended up more on his side than the other. Not that I could ever get as passionate about it as he did. I'm just not that way when it comes to big things. And not that I let on anything to my husband, either. By then I had learned how not to rock the boat. Still, I felt stronger just for having an opinion.

"I also tried not to get involved in the parish hassle over Ted's ideas. As long as you just went there, made your communion and left, you didn't notice it. But as soon as you began to look like one of the regulars, the recruiting drive started. First, the ones who were all for him, with things to sign and meetings for this and that. Always a big pitch, as if obviously there was only one side to be on. Then the others, not so pushy, just sort of testing you out to see if you were one of them. I landed in the middle, I guess. Neither side was sure they had me, so they both kept trying. At any rate, as I made friends, I wound up with some of each, and didn't say what I thought people didn't want to hear. Maybe that sounds two-faced, but it was getting to be second nature with me. Anyway it worked. It even made me a little mysterious. Which was nice."

"You sound more political than you give yourself credit for being."

"Maybe. It doesn't matter now."

"How long was it before you got to know him well?"

"I had been there about a year before he got to be really aware of me. At least as far as I know, that's when it began for him. I knew where I stood about him long before that, even at a distance. But I never thought anything would come of it. Even when he started calling on me more often—about the beginning of the second year—I didn't think anything. At first he came once a month or so. He seemed to enjoy talking to someone who wasn't so obviously turned on or turned off. They weren't exactly intellectual conversations. He was a lot more intelligent than I am, and I couldn't always follow him. But he was easy to talk to, and there were a lot of things like nature, and walking, and children, and marriage—kind of life things—that we could spend hours on without even realizing it. I guess his love just grew by itself, underneath. He never did anything about in an obvious way. After a while he started touching me more often, but it was hard to tell what that meant to him. I was the one who upset the applecart."

"How so?"

"He came to visit on my birthday. He didn't know that it was, but I was feeling good and being funny, and he asked why. So I told him, and when he wanted to know how old I was, I made him guess. He aimed low on purpose and said late twenties, and I said, 'Thank you, Sir.' He guessed wrong two more times, so I finally told him, thirty-two. Then he said, 'What would you really like for a birthday present?' Just for fun, I said, 'I've always wanted to kiss a man with a beard.' He said, 'Here's one,' and I kissed him and that was it. It all poured out. The next visit was wild. The one after that, we were in bed. He phoned every day and came at least once a week. By that time, I was keeping the attendance records for his Church School—he had asked me to teach, but that wasn't for me—so he always had some little business reason for showing up. But the reasons were mostly for his benefit.

Once he started coming often, I didn't need them, and never asked why.

"It's easier for a woman, I think. Falling in love, I mean. He took a long time to admit it, and maybe he never did really accept it. At least, he never got over having to have reasons. Even when he stopped bothering with the little bits of business, he had to go on justifying what we were doing on the basis of how important it was and how much it meant to him. I just realized one day that I only cared that he was there. It sounds funny, but almost as soon as I met him, I just looked at his lips once, while he was talking and knew I was falling in love with him. Do you believe in love at first sight?"

"It doesn't matter whether you believe in it or not. It happens. Maybe it's easier for women in general, but I don't think you can make out a case that's always the truth. I've heard men say just what you said. Including the part about their being the ones who didn't need reasons. But you're probably right. Men seem to need them more often."

"Well, I just didn't. But with him, it was always a problem. Not that he wasn't really in love with me. A woman knows. And when we were together, he was wonderful. Especially if we didn't actually make love—which seemed like most of the time, what with three children taking turns being home from school sick, and all summer with someone in the house. When we made love, though, he would get very moody and guilty-feeling afterward, and for days, sometimes weeks, he would go on about how he didn't like the idea of being unfaithful to his wife.

"That was the hardest part to take. All that talk about being fair to her but not wanting to hurt me either. It was just horrible. As long as he felt good about loving me, he would call me almost every day, but when he felt guilty there would be one big phone call that went on for hours about how breaking it off was the only thing to do. And then no more calls at all.

"For about the first year of that I would cry and get angry and carry on, and he would tell me he couldn't stand me leaning on him. And do you know what the worst thing was? It was just at those times, when he was saying goodbye for good, that he couldn't even say he loved me. Which was the only thing I wanted to hear. I knew he did, but knowing it doesn't mean much when someone won't say it.

"The break-offs never lasted, though. By and by there would be another phone call, or he would drop by, and it would start all over again, better than ever. As I said, that whole year, I made a lot of mistakes. Whenever it got good again, I would think he was over being guilty, and I'd ask him to meet me somewhere just to be alone with him. Well, sometimes he could manage that. Then I would start pressing for a little more. Like meeting me for a drink in some other town. Why is it that men don't understand that even when a woman knows love has to be a secret, she still aches for it to be public somehow? It's so easy to do, really. Even for him. Especially for him. I used to tell him, get in the habit of meeting other women in public. Take your secretary out for a drink before Christmas. Doesn't anybody ever want to see you without her husband or her family or her neighbors knowing she has a problem? It sounds scheming, but it's so easy.

"Anyway, before I finally came to my senses, I got him to meet me in New York at a hotel one afternoon. I even went in early and registered for the room myself, which I'd never done before, just to make it easier for him. I made up a big chatty story for the desk clerk about having to meet my husband later and how he wasn't sure whether we would have to fly to Chicago that afternoon or stay overnight in New York till morning—all just to explain why I was paying the bill cash in advance.

"I went up to the room and waited. I wasn't even sure he would come. But finally, an hour late, he phoned and said he'd be along in twenty minutes. When he got there, he was a nervous wreck, looking up and down the hall, and wanting to leave the minute he got in the room. I tried to be as calm as I could and eventually we made love. But he was so rattled, it was over as soon as it started, and then I knew it was all a big mistake. Yes, he loved me. Yes, it was wonderful. No, he wasn't sorry. He was only sorry for being shaky when I was so great. It was just that if he didn't leave now, he would get caught in traffic and have to explain why he was late. And no, he really wanted to leave alone, because he was nervous, so would I please understand. And all that while he was getting dressed. Then he left. Just like that.

"The first thing I did was cry. Mostly, I think, from

frustration. But then I got angrier with him than I ever was before or since. Where did he get off laying his nervousness on me? I was sick of being the dumping ground for his guilt. What did he do? He came to the city with legitimate business, did it, got caught in traffic, and got home late. I was the one who had to make the phony shopping trip. I was the one who had to pay the clerk while I was scared to death of being arrested for prostitution. I was the one who had left home so early that the rush hour would be no excuse. I was the one with the cast-iron emotions, who always had to give in when he couldn't take it.

"I was furious. With him, and with myself for getting that open to a man again. I never knew I could be that angry with anyone I loved. The whole year of putting up with it just came pouring out of me. Waiting for phone calls that never came. Not being able to call him unless it had been two or three weeks since I last called. And then hearing him so stiff and nervous and loud, talking for the benefit of everybody else in the house, when probably none of them were paying attention anyhow.

"But when you really love someone, the anger finally runs out, and you're left with the love. Which is the worst thing of all, because you know you've finally pushed too hard, and this time it really is the end. And you go all cold with fear. You don't wish you were dead. You are dead. For a while, there's a little flicker of hope and you pray with all your might for one more chance, but you know there won't be one, and you die again.

"I never did anything sadder than getting dressed alone in that room. Do you know what it's like, putting back on the clothes he took off you, when you're sure he'll never make love to you again? I don't remember anything except that sadness. Not leaving the room, not going down in the elevator, not walking twelve blocks to the parking garage. I can't even remember if I took the bridge or the tunnel. I was a zombie. The first thing I recall is passing a Holiday Inn halfway out the Expressway. That was where I suggested meeting him before he decided it was too close and told me to go to New York instead. Then I got a little anger back. And a little life. Not furious anger, like the first. Just dull, hard anger. Not even so much at him. Just at God or Life, I guess. But at least it got me home able to think up an explanation and fake the time from dinner to bed. But then I thought about what a waste my good excuse was, and the sadness came back worse than ever. I had to go to sleep without crying so my husband wouldn't guess. He never did, you know. It all worked perfectly, except that it would never work again at all.

"Well, this time I knew he wouldn't call, not even to tell me it had to be broken off. And he didn't. I stayed away from church, kept busy around the house and walked for hours on the beach. My cure again. Well, gradually it helped a little, and when things finally got to the point where I just had to get those attendance records caught up, I figured I might as well stop pretending he wasn't there and face it.

"I went to the parish office—there were always people around—and picked up the teachers' cards. I was just leaving when he came out of his office. 'Wait a second,' he said, 'I'll walk you out.' When we got outside he said, 'This isn't going to work either. I love you. Go home. I'll phone you.'

"That was it. I tore home with tears in my eyes, saying, 'Oh God, thank you,' over and over and over, and promising myself never to lean on him again—which, believe it or not, I really didn't. Except maybe once or twice, in small ways that didn't seem to matter.

"I was in the house one minute before the phone rang. He said, 'Look, please forgive me. Either for what I did or for what I'm doing now, whichever. I have to see you again.' And I said, 'Ted, I just love you. I have no choice. When do you want to come?' And he said, 'Right now, but your kids will be home in ten minutes. How about tomorrow noon?'

"We talked till the children got off the bus. I told him I would try not to lean, that I understood what I had done to him, and that all I cared about was him, not any particular way he came. And he told me he was through being nervous, and that if it came to living with guilt or without me, the guilt was the thing that had to be sacrificed. I was alive again."

She sat back, took a deep breath, exhaled, and didn't breathe in for several seconds.

"The rest is history. As far as I could see, the love got quieter and harder, but better. As if we had both decided to be very careful for each other. It was a long time before we slept together again. And over the four years since then, it didn't happen all that often. In the middle of it, my husband finally found himself a girl friend. It took him exactly three weeks, start to finish, to get shacked up in Wheeling, West Virginia. At first I was furious. Mr. Morality. He gets one chance and bolts. After all those years of beating up on me for turning down better chances than he ever dreamed of. After a while, though, I calmed down. Whoever got him deserved him. Maybe she might even do him some good. Anyway, he was gone. He sent money, mostly when he felt like it, and Ted could come in the evenings sometimes.

"That was hard, too, but I just swallowed it. Even when you get rid of the aggravation and find yourself free, it isn't the same as having a man around the house. A woman needs more than a lover, I think. There's this girl in my neighborhood who's big on Women's Lib. To hear her talk, there ought to be dancing in the street every time a man walks out on his wife. I don't agree with that. She's got a husband at home. She doesn't know what it's like to go to bed alone while your lover goes home to his wife.

"But anyway, aside from that, it was mostly good, especially, I thought, for him. He did actually seem better. He certainly said he was better. But ever since his death, I've had this terrible feeling that maybe I was some kind of disease to him. One of those things where you have it for a while, and then the symptoms go away, but the disease is really still there all along. What do you call that?"

"A remission. You get them in multiple sclerosis."

"That's right. Those last four years were a remission. Maybe if I'd said No outside his office that day, he would have been cured."

"Did you get any hints that he was thinking of suicide?"

"No. None at all. But maybe that was only self-centeredness. Maybe I just assumed that it was no harder for him to swallow his guilt than it was for me to not lean. I just don't know. Maybe his guilt was a slow poison, and without me, he wouldn't have had it in him. Do you think so?"

"It's impossible to say. Since his funeral, I've talked to most of the people who were close to him. If it's any comfort, none of them had any more suspicion than you that he could even think of such a thing."

She leaned forward and put her face in her hands.

"Do you realize that's no comfort at all? I loved him. In spite of all the trouble, I really thought I was one of the things that held him together, that gave him somewhere to be, somewhere to find himself. Do you have any idea what it's like to love somebody that much and then have to think you never understood at all how really alone they were?"

"It's bad. I haven't talked to anybody who hasn't got some guilt about him that can't be pinned down. Including me. I knew him fairly well. Not as a close friend—I supposed we were too much different breeds of cat—but we were thrown together quite a bit. The Friday before he died, I was with him at a diocesan committee meeting. The conversation at lunch was all good-natured small talk. Nobody picked up a thing."

I remember thinking it would be better if she cried. She just put her palms against her cheeks and stared at the floor.

"You know, sometimes when we were talking on the phone, somebody in his house would start to come into the room where he was, and he would say very formally, 'Well, thanks for calling. Bye.' And he'd hang up. Just like that. Do you know what that's like? You're deathly afraid that something has gone wrong, that his wife or somebody caught on, and you panic because you can't call back to find out. And there's nothing to do but wait, maybe for days. And while you wait, sometimes you ache to love him and sometimes you're angry at him for throwing your love away just because he wasn't calm enough to do the sensible thing and bluff it out. Well, suicide is the same thing, a hundred times worse. With the phone, at least you could eventually call back sometime. Or else he would. This is like being hung up on forever. I thought I'd gotten over my anger at him, but if I'm honest, I have to admit it's still there. Right along with the love. How can anyone who loves you hurt you so much?"

Her palms still against her face, she rocked herself back and forth with a small, unconscious motion. I almost started to say something about the crucifixion, but for some questions, even a good answer is wrong. The only correct reply to 'My God, my God, why have you forsaken me?' is total silence.

I leaned over and ran the back of my hand against the back of hers. Physical contact seemed meaningless. Love made to a dead virgin. She straightened, let her fingertips slide down the sides of her neck, breathed out heavily and dropped her hands into her lap.

"I made a promise. Once, when we were talking, he said that if I ever died, he thought he would probably have to tell somebody, somewhere, how he had loved me, because it would be unbearable not to. But another time, when I said the same thing about myself, he was in a different mood and asked me please not to because of other people. I suppose it was one of those silly romantic conversations in which you get all serious about death, but only because at the time it's impossible to take it seriously. But anyway, I promised him I wouldn't, and I honestly think I could have kept it, if it had been any other kind of death.

"Do you know? When I came in here, I was pretty sure talking to you was the right thing to do, and I guess it helped a little. But now, the broken promise is just one more sadness. When does it end?"

"Maybe, at least, that will be the last new sadness. In any case, it's not the main thing. All of your failures and all of his, all piled together, can't possibly matter as much as the love, unless you insist on them. What you did has got to be kept more important than anything you did wrong. I really believe that. Somehow, God gets it all reconciled in the end, and the main thing comes out on top."

"I know that. I just can't see it."

"It doesn't matter. If that's true, then everything is already reconciled, no matter how it seems. Listen, if you ever want to talk some more—even just talk—feel free to call. It's not just a one-way street, you know."

She stood up quickly.

"Yes," she said. "Thanks."

Undecipherable.

Office door. Front door. Steps.

"See you."

"See you."

Wave.

IV

Friday, April 27th

Let me go back a little.

The first word I had of his death came late on a Wednesday morning. I had called the Bishop's office to check on the dates of a lecture series I was supposed to give, and, as usual, his secretary's list didn't agree with mine. We straightened it out. Had I heard about Father Jacobs? No, I hadn't. He had been killed in an automobile accident in the middle of the night. The Bishop was on his way out there.

I called Terry Hamilton, the priest of the parish next to his. He knew. Ted's wife had phoned him about two in the morning, right after the police told her he had been killed. He had gone over, stayed for an hour, and offered to go to the undertaker's with her in the morning. She didn't know any details. When he got home, he called the Nassau County Police. Yes, he was Anne Jacobs's

EXIT 36

pastor; when did it happen? 12:30 A.M. Where? Northern State Parkway, westbound, Exit 36. Sunnyside Boulevard. How? His car hit the bridge abutment at eighty miles an hour. Eighty! He never drove like that; what was it, a mechanical failure or something? No, Father, it was suicide; there was a note. Where was the body? Syosset Hospital, D.O.A. Very badly cut up.

Terry had just come back from taking Anne over to Conklin's. The funeral was set for 11:00 A.M. Friday. Cremation. Private burial. Churchyard at St. James.

I'VE HAD TO pick up the pieces after suicides, too. They're all bad. Quick or slow, it makes no difference. Guns, pills, it doesn't matter. Dead is dead. Unexplained is unexplained. There's nobody to blame, no smallest tatter of causality or reason with which to clothe the mind's ignorance. Just sudden death itself, naked and without notice. One thunderclap out of a starry sky; then, nothing. Patricia Donahue was right. The receiver is just slammed down forever. The phone is not unlisted or off the hook. It's out of order world without end.

Yet the drawn-out methods are worse, somehow. I know Northern State Parkway by heart. Two, sometimes three trips a week to Garden City. *Exit 36 is halfway in.* The first two overpasses are right at the beginning, after Veterans' Highway. The next one is at Sagtikos. The next two come after Deer Park Avenue and Wolf Hill Road. Then two more before Route 110. Then Sunnyside Boulevard.

When do you write the note? Do you decide in advance which bridge you will hit? If not, how many times do you decide it won't be this one, but the next? And what do you think of? Do you think about your kids? Or do you turn on the radio to avoid thinking about them? Are you angry, or just out of your head? When do you floor the accelerator? Are you tempted to swerve at the last minute? If so, how many times?

THE DAY OF the funeral, I drove south on Route 112 to Coram. Godawful Long Island main roads! Ugly quick-food stands, followed by corny shopping plazas, followed by flashy VW dealerships, followed by filthy oil-truck depots. Rivers of beer cans and plastic trashbags, flowing past the last ratty patches of woods left after Mr. Levitt *et al.* bulldozed in their chintzy enormities: Birchwood at Sagamore Hills; Strathmore East. Twenty-five years ago, this was country. I used to drive down here to take the rubbish to the Coram Pit. Now my buried garbage, risen and glorified, covers the earth.

Turned left at Jericho Turnpike. Route 25, the Mississippi of uglification to which 112 is a mere tributary. Even twenty-five years ago it was bad. Now? Words fail. Long Island has been destroying itself, west to east, for three hundred years. Something in the soul of its people that makes real estate God and then offers only sleazy sacrifices. Grant Plaza, Robert Hall. Nothing ever built well. Nothing ever torn down or cleaned up, unless something worse can be done. New and garish, old and shabby—shocking pink cheek by sagging, unshaven jowl—mile after mile after mile. No care for the whole; therefore nothing but despicable parts. No priestly offerings for the sake of the City; therefore only Black Masses of self-destruction. Long Island as the grand sacrament of the sickness in the American air. Maybe that's what he died of. Maybe my survival is only a remission.

East for a mile, then north again to the church. Better. Side road. I'm on time, but the parking lot is jammed and I have to park way down the road past the church. A hundred cars? The old have modest funerals; when the young go, you can fill Shea Stadium. Something right about that. More people to cry, if they have the nerve. Jeremy Taylor said a dry funeral was a shame. A small one is a double sadness.

Long walk back. The church seats three hundred easily, but I can't get past the vestibule. Lots of priests, maybe sixty or eighty. The Bishop, Terry Hamilton, and a seminary classmate of Ted's are concelebrating the mass. White vestments. White pall on the coffin.

When I was a new priest, you wore black for a requiem. Grim. Even for the faithful departed, you sang the *Dies irae*. "Day of wrath, O day of mourning": the Good News of Salvation, musically arranged to scare the hell out of you. And for the unfaithful departed—for those who had "laid violent hands upon themselves"—you weren't even allowed to use that. In place of the regular rite, you were supposed to piece together something which would give as much comfort as possible to the living, consistent with your obligation to remain conspicuously noncommittal about the fate of the deceased. Most of us at least had the grace to be embarrassed. We used the Prayer Book rite anyway. Still, we felt obliged to explain to ourselves that it was really all right because, who knows, maybe Uncle Arthur got in a couple of seconds' worth of repentance between the Brooklyn Bridge and the river. That worked until you found out he shot himself. Then it was time to hunt for another rationalization. Unbelievable! As if the bits of ethical brickwork just before the edge of the abyss were more important than the dead Christ at the bottom. Damned nonsense! The reconciliation of all things in heaven and earth made subsidiary to nitpicking about the last-minute state of some poor bastard's conscience. Where did the church get her knack for putting the main thing last? Her genius for Solemn High Distractions?

The mass is mostly a mumble from where I stand, so I move outside to the steps. Three priests, all friends of mine, smoking. What did I know? Was it really suicide? Yes, the note was clear enough. What did it say? Didn't see it. As far as I knew, even Terry Hamilton didn't. The notes never tell you much anyway.

Quiet, tentative speculation.

"It just doesn't fit Ted. He was such a gentle guy. Suicide is nasty, angry business."

"I heard the parish was giving him a bad time. All these transplanted Archie Bunkers out here. Suffolk County is the heaven they go to after they've passed their probation as good Queens Republicans. They probably put him in the same category as crabgrass."

"That's right. He was gentle enough, but he was always spreading. He never let up."

"Still, that's not enough of a reason. He didn't seem to be falling apart over it all. Last Friday at lunch, he seemed fine."

"I don't know about that. What was that business about his thinking the bay scallops tasted fishy? I tasted them. They were perfectly fresh."

"Beats me. What's that supposed to be? Some kind of pre-psychotic symptom?"

"Could be."

"You've all got the blame in the wrong place. We're to blame. The clergy of this diocese are the most cut-up, competitive, paranoid group on earth. We're so estranged from each other that no help ever comes in time. All we do is gossip when it's too late."

"What good is trying to fix the blame? I'm going in and make my communion. At least it's something to do."

"Me too."

I SAID A mass for him earlier, so I stay outside. Bright, warm sun. But somewhere, right in the middle of the light, the emptiness of his sheer nonbeing. Communion drags on and on. The choir sings "Jesus, Son of Mary":

> Rest eternal grant them, After weary fight;
> Shed on them the radiance, Of thy heavenly light.

> Lead them onward, upward, To thy holy place,
>   Where thy saints made perfect, Gaze upon thy face.

Is that really right? It's better than the psychologizing and the attempts to assign guilt, but isn't it just another distraction? Nothing matters right now but the darkness of Ted's death. I don't really want to hear that somewhere, out where it's light, Christ is going to do a great job on him some day. I want to hear what Christ is doing now with the nothing he now is. We stand around and fish for explanations, as if Ted's having done something unexplainable were the problem—as if one shrewd analysis would solve it all. But the problem is not anything he did. The problem is what he is: He's dead.

And for that problem, if I'm honest, there is no solution. What in God's name is the point of having to become nothing after you've actually been somebody? I know the answers. But they're all too slick. Like death being part of the natural process, or a doorway into larger life. Or death being the soul's liberation to go from strength to strength until the risen body catches up with it at the day of judgment. You know what's wrong with that? It puts the main thing last again. It puts coping with the Mystery ahead of the Mystery itself. Don't solve my problems by telling me death is a good idea, death is a step up. And don't talk to me about some philosophical distinction called my soul. Talk about me. Because death is my enemy. Death kills me. Death makes my love naught. Tell me otherwise, and I'll know you never loved.

And above all, don't tell me Christ is risen from the dead and therefore death is a pussycat. The hope of the resurrection, put that way, is the biggest distraction of all. It skirts the operative heart of the Mystery: Jesus' death. If Jesus is God, then everything he does is forever. If he is risen forever, *he is also dead forever.* Tell me what that means. Tell me why God has to be the Lamb slain from the foundation of the world. Don't hand me some perpetually playful kitten; give me the great, eternally dead Lion of the tribe of Judah. Don't talk me around the Mystery. Talk me through it. And don't tell me it's silly to be angry with the surest thing in the world. I know that, but I'm still angry. So was Job. God has got to be doing something with the unending blackness of his own death and mine; otherwise, the whole thing is just a stupid arrangement which even a two-bit creator would have had the sense to straighten up.

THE COFFIN IS carried in procession to the hearse. Easter hymn: "The strife is o'er, the battle done." With alleluias, yet. Maybe the old, gloomy requiem mass was better. Not that this isn't true; just that it's too fast. We are looking away from something huge and speechless before we've given it a chance to make the sign we need to see. Still, the music is marvelous: Palestrina. Three of us standing together sing bass; two priests across the sidewalk belt out the tenor. "Lord, by the stripes which wounded thee, From death's dread sting, thy servants free, That we may live and sing to thee. Alleluia." Great. The cadence at the Amen, however, is not the usual plagal one. Instead, it goes from the tonic to the key of the dominant. The ones who know the music confuse the ones who don't, and the whole effort collapses in embarrassment. Even the distraction points to itself and says it is a distraction.

AT THE END, a few of us stood around talking. To everyone's credit, nobody offered any cheap funeral-parlor theology. All that was left was the sense of robbery that always comes with sudden death. Totally successful, totally futile robbery. The goods are not just missing, they are destroyed. Looking for the culprit is either pointless or terrifying: If it's something or somebody on earth, he hasn't got them either; and if it's God, then we have yet to face the depth of his complicity in our destruction.

Some other day though, not now.

"Why don't you swing up to Port and drop by for a drink? There's braunschweiger and ham ends if you're hungry."

Two takers.

Life again. While the darkness waits for us, we shall have diocesan politics at noon, and later, maybe make some parish calls. With luck, lunch will last till it's too late to make the calls.

V

Wednesday, May 2nd

I DIDN'T GO to the funeral parlor when he was laid out. On principle. I never go near them unless I have to. Not because I don't want to face death. Just the reverse: The entire American funeral establishment is dedicated to the scrupulous avoidance of facing it. Forest Lawn is no aberration; it is the crowning expression of a philosophy: Death as non-event, for whose setting a non-world must be provided. The most authentically molar reality in life is tucked into a parenthesis of tufted satin and surrounded with imitation everything. Imitation colonial architecture, imitation Gainsborough paintings, imitation religious music, and above all, imitation language. The Pentagon didn't invent it; they borrowed it from the undertakers. The corpse is never called a corpse; even "body" is too coarse for comfort. Nor is the loved one "laid out"; he reposes. And not in the room on the left;

rather, in Chapel B, or in the Wedgwood Room.

And at the grave—located in a Memorial Park, not a cemetery—the dirt, which is always called earth, is covered with imitation grass mats. No shovelful is thrown, however. The priest, unless he kicks back the corner of the mat and gets himself a handful of real clay and pebbles, is provided by the funeral director, *né* undertaker, with a purple-and-silver cardboard salt shaker filled with fine, with sand.

And every day of every year, real people with real grief over really dead relatives go right along with it. In my whole life, I have been to honest, death-facing funeral rites under only two circumstances. Between our fourth and fifth child, we had twins: Grace and Paul. Grace was stillborn, strangled by the umbilical cord. I asked the Friars at Little Portion if I could have a small plot in their cemetery and told the undertaker I would take care of things myself. A brother priest came over. We said a Mass of the Angels and then went and dug the grave ourselves.

Paul had a congenital heart defect and died twenty-four hours later. Same arrangement, except this time my two sons, seven and five, undertook with me. We talked while we worked in the August heat. Make the bottom level. How long will it take for the box to rot? Is the dirt piled high enough to end up level after it collapses? There. Is that smooth enough? We mopped our foreheads, read the rite for the Burial of a Child, and tramped back to the Friary barn with the farm shovels over our shoulders. Do you know how I felt? Human.

The other kind of funeral I put in the same class is the burial of a priest or a religious according to the old custom. Too bad Ted's wasn't done that way. I hope mine is. First of all, you are buried in mass vestments; one of your brother priests has to vest your corpse to make sure the job gets done right. I haven't had to do that yet, but unless I'm the first in my class called up, the job is waiting for me. Then too, you're laid out in the chancel of the church and a vigil is set up till the requiem. Priests and others take an hour or so apiece all through the night and day, so that there is no time when there isn't somebody there. Finally, your pallbearers are real friends, not paid flunkies.

All that, I've done. Including being at the right rear corner of the coffin of a Mother Superior who must have spent the last twenty years eating a whole Whitman's Sampler every day and then crashed through the floor of her cell at four hundred pounds. The M.C. had no talent for engineering and arranged us so that the two short priests were in the middle. Their shoulders just grazed the bottom. Mine hurt for a week.

The only honest distraction from death—the only one that won't sicken your soul or rot your theology—is having something to do. People survive the idiocy we put them through only because, apart from the idle fakery of the obsequies, they really are busy: phoning relatives, getting money out of the joint account in a hurry, turning couches into beds for relatives they haven't seen since the wedding, feeding an army, and drinking themselves properly silly. For the record, in addition to giving me the full treatment in church, I hope my family has the sense to have me laid out beforehand in the front parlor, and to have four cases—one Scotch, one Bourbon, one Gin and one Madeira—laid in, in the cellar. That done, they may cross themselves and get on with the party in the back room. Just to make sure, however, I put down here, for my wife's eyes, a truth I know will etch itself on her mind: *They don't allow liquor in funeral parlors.* There! When you hear I am dead, come to the house.

VI

Wednesday, May 2nd

T HE UPSHOT OF my aversion to the burying business was that I didn't pay a personal call on Ted's wife until the week after the funeral. I had known Anne for the eight years they had been in Coram, but not as well as I knew him. Once or twice, we had them both up for a drink in the evening. Now and then I would see her at meetings. Some years ago, I was in their rectory about once a week for three months.

In addition to his other causes, Ted was very much involved in trying to get low-income housing into the area. My social conscience is not exactly of the firebrand variety; warm glow would be a more accurate description—and perhaps even that's kinder than I deserve. My head is in the right place, but I experience difficulties getting my body to go with it to zoning-board meetings.

By sheer persistence, though, Ted finally conned me

into climbing on his low-income bandwagon. The project eventually foundered, as I thought it would all along. The hordes of middle-income troops who so recently fought their way across the Suffolk County line into the promised land were, as I saw it, simply not about to send engraved invitations to their less fortunate former neighbors in Brooklyn.

While the push was on, though, Ted's house was headquarters for the weekly strategy meetings. Anne was in on it all with him. They had been married before he went to seminary—right after she graduated from Middlebury, I think. At any rate, they were intellectually and socially two of a kind. It was one of those clerical marriages which most people consider ideal. I didn't know them in their seminary days, but I knew lots like them. Earnest. Together. Lots of talk about "our" ministry. Long discussions of large subjects. Couples sitting cross-legged on the floor till two A.M., with gallons of coffee, hardly any wine, and no whiskey at all. Car? VW, of course. The car for people of principle, right or left. The great American monstrance of conviction, the true vehicle of the bumper sticker: P.O.W.s NEVER HAVE A NICE DAY. McGOVERN FOR PRESIDENT. Old Glory and Flower Power.

I suppose what I'm saying is that, however admirable all their earnestness was, I was never really comfortable in the presence of it. Maybe it's a flaw in my character, but I found it—well, dull. More likely though, it's just a matter of temperament. I come from a line of story-telling whiskey drinkers. I like my sincerities short, and liberally laced with Scotch while they last. I would come home from their place after three hours of seriousness *cum* black coffee and lie awake half the night.

I have a theory that people who can pour that much coffee into their systems must have a fundamentally "low" physical and psychological make-up. Ten cups of coffee just bring them up to normal; two whiskies knock them flat. My own type, on the other hand, is fundamentally "high": I need a fearful amount of depressant before I'm depressed. One full bottle of (preferably good) wine makes me a perfect lunch before a normal afternoon. Three coffees, and my hands tremble.

The theory is probably false as often as it's true, but it held up in the case of Anne and Ted. As I said, when we first met them, we invited them up for drinks. Liz and I, however, are just about as evenly matched on the high side as they were on the low, so after about two tries, there simply were no more invitations. Not that it was discussed; just tacitly given up on.

And not that Anne wasn't attractive. She was quite tall and, without being skinny, had a nice, lean look about her. She had the resources for making a sexual impression, but somehow, to me at least, she just didn't. At first glance, you assumed she would be a show worth watching. But you could watch as long as you liked: She just never came on. She had a good mind and could argue for hours, but unfortunately, after all the talk there was just no fun in here at all. They never got on the New Year's Eve party list.

Ted, on the other hand, was a lot more alive to his sexuality. Not that he wasn't reserved; sometimes he was positively stiff. But you sensed that, with him, it was a matter of holding back, not a case of nothing doing. I don't think he was quite aware of it himself, but when he felt good, he courted women fairly obviously. He was capable of small talk with no other purpose than coming on strong. Liz picked that up right away, and I saw it at meetings and dances.

He was also handsome. I never saw him without the beard—I think that, clean-shaven, he would have had a weak chin—but with it, he was gorgeous: a straight, strong face with a magnificent chestnut-brown flourish, scissor-trimmed to a neat three or four inches, but never touched by a razor. Nature had provided him free with what the rest of us have to work for. Just the right balance between face and hair: not too high on the cheekbones or too low on the neck. In vestments, he looked positively apostolic.

If I had known, when Pat Donahue first phoned, that he had been involved with her, it would have made no sense at all. For him to tumble to somebody who pronounced her name "Patreesha" would have been inconceivable. As it was though, when she finally appeared in person and dropped the shoe, it wasn't that hard to figure. Even with all the burners off, she was on. He probably wasn't used to quite that much, but he instinctively knew the signals. This was no coffee girl with a used VW in the garage. This was Seagram's 7 and ginger, with a Pontiac convertible in the parking lot. She was a lot more than that, too, no doubt; but she was unmistakably, exactly, that: Body English spoken here. At home, I guess, they spoke mostly Sociologese.

I DROVE DOWN on the back roads, just to avoid 112. When I got to the rectory, the place was as full of people as ever. I never did meet the crowd in the kitchen. Anne was in the living room with Dick Jorjorian, one of Ted's vestrymen—a county welfare supervisor whom I knew from the housing meetings. There were also her brother Laurence, a lawyer, and Ted's sister, Joan. I hadn't met either. Introductions.

"I just wanted to drop by and say hello. If I'm interrupting, say so. I have no pearls to drop. At least, not any you could cash in."

"That's all right. We're all pitching in on the subject of what I do next. Dick and Larry are all for my staying put for a while. Dick says there's no rush about moving."

"There really isn't, Anne. Even at high speed, it'll be months before we're ready to elect anybody. We haven't even begun to talk about it. You could stay at least through the summer."

"I know, Dick, but the more I think about it, the more I think I'd rather do it sooner than later."

Church-owned clergy housing. A vestige of the good old days that ought to be operated on. Admittedly, I live in a bigger house than I could ever afford: seventeen fun-filled rooms, some of them with hundred-year-old plaster on (or off) the walls. But the real mischief is that when I retire, I don't have one cent of equity in the place. And if I die in harness, my widow has no mortgage insurance. Therefore no way of getting title to anything. My shrewder priest friends nowadays either buy their own houses and have the church make the payments, or insist that the vestry take out life insurance on them sufficient to give their wives the equivalent of mortgage insurance. Ted didn't have either. Neither do I. He was too idealistic to think of it, and I'm too lazy to push for it. Still, it's a smart idea, and mostly for Dick's benefit, I lay it out briefly. For Anne, it's all water over the dam; but there'll be another time for somebody. There's no reason to perpetuate a system which amounts to an involuntary vow of poverty.

We went back to the subject of moving. She thought she would stay until the children were out of school, and look around meanwhile for a small place to buy. Various towns mentioned. I gathered she wanted to stay in Suffolk but didn't think too much of living in Coram. Some place near the shore, perhaps. Money didn't seem to be a problem.

Her brother. John Lindsay type. Bishop Paul Moore minus the clericals and fifteen years. What is there about old WASP money that produces tall offspring who, after Philips Exeter and Yale, lean to the left? When he spoke to her, he used what I assumed was a family nickname—at least I never heard Ted use it:

"Nan, don't move too fast. July at the very earliest.

And don't jump at the first place you think you like. There isn't that much of Suffolk County that I would call your cup of tea. When you start to decide, call me, and I'll come out."

I threw in something about giving a damaged plant time to mend its tissue in place before transplanting it.

Ted's sister, Joan, sat up stiffly and looked at both of us. "I'm sure that Anne will do just fine once she gets the legal profession off her back. And the church."

Her delivery was colorless, but it garrotted the whole subject. The part about the legal profession might have been her idea of banter, but the part about the church came out as a verdict of guilty.

I ducked. Originally, I had thought that the subject of Ted's death might somehow come up, but, with his sister in the room, that obviously was not going to be a pleasant experience, especially for me. Too much voltage in all those wires down there in the dark. Don't touch. Start hunting for the exit.

Anne stood up. She really did appreciate all the concern. Everybody had been marvelous. Why didn't she get us some coffee? It would only take a minute.

There it was.

"No thanks, Anne, I really have to run. Let me know if I can do anything. I have a couple of real estate people in the parish. Give me a ring. Dick, great to see you again. Joan, Larry, good to meet you. Anne, take care."

Out.

VII

Friday, May 11th

THE MORE I think about Ted and about myself, the more I feel the distance between us. Individual lives are such provincial pieces of business. We operate day to day on the assumption that we are more like the next fellow than we are unlike him; but that's never true in the clutches. And we get into the clutches precisely because we assumed it was. We land, intelligibly enough, in business or in bed, because the dimensions of our lives—we were both lawyers, or romantics, or chess players, or oversexed—trick us into believing that those neat congruities pierce to the marrow and discern the heart. But they hardly even graze the skin. They remain only dimensions—external, arbitrary sizings-up of a mystery fundamentally and forever alien to themselves. The huge, dumb thing they measure—myself—pays them no mind. It may, in hectic office or torrid bed, remain politely out of sight; but at three o'clock on some lonely, sleepless night, it barges rudely in, sweeps aside the sociable parentheses in which I have so far explained myself to myself, and stupidly presents itself as the main text—in Chinese: "My God! She doesn't really know me at all!" And neither do I.

On the surface, Ted and I were not so far apart. For practical purposes, we were commensurable enough: Two boys from Queens who went to city high schools, read the *New York Times*, voted democratic, and were ordained to the priesthood by the same bishop. Ten years apart in age, of course, and different personality types; but sufficiently congruent for the differences to be taken in stride—for me to assume they were only a matter of salt in the mashed potatoes. I didn't find him grossly excessive or totally lacking, so I simply swallowed and got on with it. I never treated him as something I had to fathom. I wish I had. Because now I have to fathom him in the context of the ultimate difference: I'm alive; he's dead.

He was a good parish priest. I am not, really. I am a good-enough priest, if all you expect is sermons, sacraments and an ear to bend. But if you want someone to run a high-powered operation, I am not your man. He was: lots of parish calls, dozens of church activities, plenty of hospital visits. Totally available. Hardly ever a day off. The kind of ministry people think of as ideal, and bishops praise *ad nauseam*, provided it produces bucks and buildings—which his did. He put that whole show on the boards down there in eight years. From scratch.

Oddly though (really not oddly at all, once you've

been in this business long enough), his parish gave him a hard time. Not the majority of them, of course. But there are certain types of laypeople who get their jollies by beating up on the priest. Ted had a couple of solid-brass bastards on his vestry. When a priest presents the kind of high parish profile he did, he's easy to hit. And not just for political activities. For warm, toasty, priestly ones, too. The more you give them, the more they complain about what you don't give. Call once during a ten-day hospitalization and the patient will tell his friends what a great guy you are. Go every day except Friday, Saturday and Sunday and he's sure to mention your derelictions.

A friend of mine, in a kind phrase, once described my parish as "not overministered to." My style is daily mass, a few calls, mostly on people who interest me, no activities at all unless somebody else runs them, and two hours a day kept inviolate for *skål* time. Plus two naps. Plus an hour and a half for running on the roads and lying on the grass. Plus another hour of reading the *Times*. I've been a parish priest for twenty-five years, but in all honesty, it was only at the very beginning that I tried hard to be a typical parish minister: The first time somebody tried to give me ulcers about the job was also the last. I learned to duck in one lesson. A family talent. My grandfather lived a peaceable fifty years with my grandmother by being a genius at rolling with the punches. I have a daughter who can disappear while you're talking to her—without ever leaving the room.

Ted either couldn't spot the ulcer-givers, or else he

thought ducking was a violation of his priestly vows. In any case, I always felt he handled them wrong. He was too good to them. I'm never actually a bastard; somehow, I get by without having to get rough. But I am very stubborn. I don't do anything unless I want to. I give all of them their freedom, but if they want to stay on board with me, they have to be very careful of mine. The result? I take a little bicarbonate of soda once or twice a year. Ted popped amphogels like peanuts.

Of course, I have an advantage. Sine 1955 I have not been dependent on the parish ministry for either all my income or all my satisfactions. I teach theology—which, of all things in the world, is the thing I like best to do. I am not a scholar, mind you; just a good classroom teacher. I love to think my way through the faith by talking about it. And my preaching is just my teaching, continued. It's a happy life, getting paid for your favorite pastime. A good teacher teaches himself. His students are the indispensable partners who return his serves, but it's really his game. And, even more so, a good preacher preaches to himself. I suppose that sounds self-serving, but it really isn't. Besides being honest, it also happens to be true: nobody learns anything unless the teacher is the eagerest learner in the room.

In addition to being a theologian, however—something Ted wasn't—I realize now that I am a lot of other things he wasn't either. For one thing, I am an inveterate hobbyist: cooking, woodworking, music, model-making. He was all work. I am also a reasonably adept cloakroom politician. He played all his cards face up, and, more often than not, lost. Above all, I am radically lazy, but blessed with enough discipline to work fast and hard in spurts. What I decide to do gets done, even though it's never a long time between drinks. He drank three beers a week, if he could work them into his schedule; I drink a quart of wine a day, plus—with time off only on Ash Wednesday and Good Friday.

Enough. The difference of our dimensions points away from the surface into the mystery of what each of us really is. What it all means is radically unclear. Am I better? Or worse? Or luckier? Or unluckier? Was he a fool for Christ's sake, and therefore miles ahead of me in holiness? Or was he just a fool, for Christ's sake, and miles behind in common sense? Am I welshing on my share of the Passion?

But, above all, does it matter? Is it going to make any difference that my life has been one long vacation to the priesthood while his was some kind of agony with a confused walk down the garden path at the end? What really counts? The amount of bloody sweat?—in which case, I'm out and he's in; or the certainty of the Death that finally saves us both? How are our differences finally dealt with, when, having gone beyond all dealing, we arrive at the indifferent nothing from which we sprang?

VIII

Friday, May 11th

WHETHER ANYTHING CAN be said to all that, remains to be seen. The practical point right now is that he is out of the game, and I am the one left with the pack of theological cards to be shuffled, cut and dealt.

To begin with, I'm going to make myself a promise to try to face Ted's death with as little excess mental baggage as possible. If I can get away with it, I want to start by saying that his life is over and he is dead for good. And I want to say that because it puts me on ground where I know what I'm talking about: At the very least, that's exactly how it feels—to Pat, to me, to Anne, to Joan, to everybody. If we're in an intellectual bind over death, we're not going to get out of it by squirming around in the intellectual ropes that put us there in the first place. I want to see if feeling isn't a safer guide out of the mental maze we've made.

That means, however, that for the present, I'm going to have to drop some of the standard mental security blankets: things about which we really know nothing, but which we pretend we know very well. No talk, for example, about his soul. No speculations about what it might be, or where it might have gone, or what it might be doing. Forget he had one. Better yet, assume he didn't. I didn't much need it when I dealt with him here; maybe I don't need it now that he's gone. Just talk about *him*. He's dead. Period.

Next, no talk about life after death. Because I don't know anything about that, either. When I talked about his *life* while he was here, I simply meant his history—the whole web of acts and relationships between the day of his birth and the day of his death, plus, if you like, nine months' gestation to get it going. I want to try out the proposition that if anything is going to be saved, it's got to be those selfsame thirty-eight years, not some endless succession of quasi-eternal days stretching out from the other side of the time he hit the abutment.

There are two reasons why I want to get rid of that essentially philosophical clothing of the situation. The first is that I don't think the gospel requires it. More than that, I don't even think the gospel is particularly comfortable with it, even after having worn it for nearly two thousand years. I'm not going to drag it out unless I have to. The second reason, though, is that, just taken simply as philosophical clothing, it's full of holes.

While Ted had his human being here, he was subject

to the laws of time and space. But now that he has no recognizable being at all (no flinching—that's the way it feels, at least), it isn't going to be useful to talk about the eternal being he may or may not have in terms that reek of time. If I bring in the notion of eternity at all, I want to use it full strength, in the only place it makes sense: as an attribute of God, and nothing else. I want to break the habit of imagining that it's some kind of supra-temporal, supra-spatial continuum—a sort of infinitely extended tapioca pudding, floating around out there beyond the fringes of time and space. I want to allow it to refer only to God's personal style of doing business, to his way of holding *at once*—in one, single, simple *now*—everything that all of time, from start to finish, has ever held. The trick will be, scrupulously to avoid thinking of it as if it were some strange new endless time, strung out beyond these times. I want never to let "eternal life" refer to anything but these short times themselves, as they are held by God in a different way than time holds them.

Because if you don't keep a watertight bulkhead between eternity and time, the leakage of temporality into eternity will seep into your religion and eventually sink your theology. Anything said on this side of the bulkhead must be in strict accordance with the rules of time; anything on the far side, with the rules of eternity. Thus, Ted began here in 1935 and ended here in 1973. So much, and nothing more, for the temporal Ted. But in God, who holds him eternally in one single now, there was never a time when he hadn't already thought of Ted, never a time when he hadn't already caused him to be, never a time when he hadn't already watched his foot go down on the accelerator in the act of causing himself not to be. As a matter of fact, those events, so discreetly successive here, are not successive in God at all. They are *all at once* in his eternity. They are not really, for him at least, even events. An event is something that *comes out*, turns out, happens: There was a time when it wasn't; then there was a time when it is. But God, as God, is not locked into time as we are. The act by which he causes each temporal thing to be is an eternal act. It is not something he thought of doing a very long time ago and then one day finally got around to plugging in. It is something he always does, something always present to his eternal being.

The point of my pencil, for example, broke on the capital T at the beginning of this sentence. That event had not yet happened at the time I put the period after the word *being*; now, as I put in this comma, it is all over, lost in an irretrievable past. But God, as the intimate and immediate cause of the act of being of everything involved in writing this paragraph, is simply present to all of it in his eternity. Put differently, His eternity is simultaneous with every one of the temporal events involved. Therefore, in Him, they are neither successive, nor are they happenings; they just always are.

But check the bulkhead to make sure it's watertight: Eternity must not be allowed to leak into time either. The only real being we have is the temporal life we live between birth and death. There is no higher life "out there" or "up there"; there is only what's here. If anything is saved, it's *this*—not something somewhere else. (I know. That doesn't sound Christian. But it is—even more so than the "great beyond" imagery I'm refusing to use. Only wait a little.)

Go back to my pencil point. Don't give it any eternal qualities. Don't start talking as if, in addition to its merely pedestrian existence here in time, it had some kind of astral or eternal existence elsewhere. That draws us off the mark we promised to aim at. The next thing you know, we'll be saying that all I really lost was the poor earthly shadow of the truer, finer pencil point in the sky. And from there it's only one step to the atrocities of the funeral parlor poet. And to sacrilege to Ted.

Repeat this after me slowly, and let its implications for your theology sink in: *Pat really loved him.* Him. The undressed, temporal thing he was. Him. The naked, perishing being which God eternally caused to be naked and perishing. You can try that ethereal nonsense on yourself if you like, but don't ever lay it on someone in her shoes. She knows what she lost. And it's not something an astral body will make shift for, now or ever: She wants *him* inside her again. Keep the feeling tap on full force. Intellectualizing is inevitable, but don't let what you think up con you into writing down things your feelings tell you are a lot for crap.

IX

Sunday, May 13th

Or into saying them in public either. After I made that more or less abrasive visit to Anne's house, I began to try to piece together my thoughts about the situation. I teach dogmatics every Saturday at the seminary. By the beginning of May, my second-year class was getting into the last topic in the curriculum—into the part of theology that hardly anyone nowadays, myself included, makes much sense of: Eschatology, the study of the Four Last Things. Death, Judgement, Hell and Heaven, together with such other winning subjects as Predestination, Election, the Resurrection of the Dead, and the Final Reconciliation of this Slugfest of a World into one Big Happy Family.

For years I had been getting more and more unhappy with the old, canned notes I had been lecturing from. So this year, when I finally couldn't stand them at all, I just winged it. The stuff in the previous chapters about getting death out in front as the main thing, and treating everything else as a distraction, comes from the first few passes I took at the subject without notes.

By the second Saturday in May, I was grappling in class with the time/eternity analysis I just gave you; and, as I do more often than not, I decided to use it for the sermon the next day. That's another bonus in my life: free, fun sermon-preparation sessions before a live audience at the school. All I have to do by myself is prepare my sermon notes at three-thirty on Sunday morning, and go back to bed when I've finished. By the time I've preached at the two masses, the material is usually in pretty good shape. When you come though, come to the ten thirty. If I make sense at all, it's then.

When I did the time/eternity bit that Sunday however, I left several bases uncovered. I leaned hard on the eternal side: how God holds our temporal lives eternally; how all you have to focus on is the threescore and ten, how, in the Christian religion, you don't need to talk about souls or the afterlife, because in him, our times are already held eternally. I used the old gag line: The question is not whether there is life after death; it's whether there's life before it. That's what God deals with.

I failed, however, to do anything much with the problem that brings up, especially for people with strong feelings. For them, the imagery of life after death serves a major purpose: It makes the promise of Christ imaginable. He says he's the resurrection and the life right now, but they are painfully aware of the fact that we all go on dying like flies nevertheless. A promise like that can seem real only if they conceive it as something which will happen in a mysterious future: Out there at the end of time, or up there beyond time, Mom and Dad really will be waiting for them. She really will have him inside her again. When you start philosophizing away that future, their feelings blow the whistle on you. You can't tell them God works only in the space between birth and death; it's just too painfully obvious to them that that's the very space in which he's not doing a damned thing—at least not anything their feelings would like. And you can't get them out of that crossrip by saying, "There, there, don't worry. He may be lost to you, but he isn't lost to God, and that's what really counts." For them, that is exactly what does not really count: it is one hell of a way to keep a promise.

At the coffee hour afterward, I got two reactions. One parishioner, who has what I think of as a bent for becoming diffusely astrological at the drop of a spiritual hat, took the line and ran with it—right into the astral-body business. She was so glad I had preached that sermon. She had always believed that we existed on two levels, and that this mortal life shouldn't concern us because our other life was the really real one. I tried to qualify my way around that, but I hadn't worked it out well enough myself, so she stayed right on her higher plane and flew home happy.

Another parishioner, however, one with her head

threaded on straight and her feeling tap in working order, spotted the real flaw in the set-up.

"That's all very well for God, you know. But it still leaves us out in the cold. If this is the only existence my sister who's dying of cancer really has, then it's not much comfort to know that God has it tucked away in some eternal pocket. If that's the best he can do, it's not good enough. It may solve his problems, but it doesn't touch her's."

I argued that I was only trying to lay aside the old imagery of the afterlife, not to welsh on any part of the promise to reconcile everything. God in Christ held her sister eternally right now, and all the pain was somehow reconciled and made right. The tears really are wiped away, not someday, but now. That at least was what I had in mind. She still wasn't buying, however:

"That may be what you meant, but it's not what I heard you say. You've got God holding my sister on two levels, one good and one horrible. But she's holding herself on only the horrible one—they've given her about six months, you know, mostly with nausea. If you're going to insist that her level is the only real one, the only one God ever deals with, then you're saying he's healing her in the very same life in which he's killing her."

I threw in something about how I could see that it was difficult to say it right, but that I still thought it was the right thing to say. It was, after all, what the crucifixion said. It was also what St. Paul said: about knowing the power of Christ's resurrection, and the fellowship of his sufferings, and being made conformable to his death, if by any means he might attain to the resurrection of the dead. Still no sale.

"But that makes more sense in the old imagery than in yours. First sufferings, then death; then afterward, at the end of the world or something, you *attain to* the resurrection of the dead."

I said No, that wasn't necessarily what it meant; that the Christian claim was that we know the power of Christ's resurrection right along with the fellowship of his sufferings; that we are baptized into his death; that we are already "dead, and our life is hid with Christ in God"—even while we're still living the only life we've got.

"Well, you should work on that part of it then. When you get philosophical you lose everybody, especially since all you really did was take away the old images. You didn't put in any new ones at least not any that gave the least hint of any real straightening up of a bad job. Don't try that on anyone in the middle of a mess until you come up with something."

I resigned the game.

"All right, so it has the glide angle of a coke bottle. Back to the drawing board."

I DIDN'T TELL you why I resigned. Until she came up to the altar rail for communion, I hadn't noticed she was in church; but when I came by with the chalice, there, under a wide-brimmed straw hat, was Pat Donahue. I didn't see her at the door afterward. She must have left right after she received.

Doing your theology out loud in public is not always fun for all concerned.

X

Monday, May 14th

I DECIDED NOT to call her—about six times over the next three days.

Mixed motives.

I think that, so far, most of the things I've told you about myself are true, apart from some necessary fictions and a couple of self-serving declarations. I am also aware that there are some things I think are true about myself which I haven't told you—and probably shouldn't. But most of the things that really are true about me, I couldn't any more tell you than keep from you. I just don't know them. At that level, we are all mysteries groping for another Mystery, compared to which our truths or falsehoods are small potatoes.

I first convinced myself that calling her was the right thing to do. Pastoral Concern. Priestly Responsibility. But then I had to question the obvious lack of even-handedness with which I dealt with the full range of my pastoral concerns: I did not spend three days debating about old Peter Anderson in the hospital. I took him communion on Monday morning, and then just didn't just get around to him until my secretary prodded me on Thursday. My concern, apparently, was slanted in the direction of fitted black and, more recently, wide-brimmed straw hats.

Next, there was a consideration of my responsibility to repair, as best I could, the spiritual damage caused by the indiscriminate distribution of half-baked theology—followed immediately by a consideration of the damage that might yet be done by a selective distribution of over-warm priest. Et cetera.

In my seminary days, as a 1947 Anglo-Catholic of the deepest dye, I studied morals from a Roman text: McHugh and Callan, O.P.—*Moral Theology. A Complete Course* (1929). The good old days, when he who hesitated was saved: all the above-mentioned problems of mixed motive, dealt with, exhaustively and exhaustingly, under the heading "The Moral System." When in doubt, look up the appropriate case of conscience in the book.

"Oh, see! See Father Titus! See Caia with a spiritual problem! See Caia walking her spiritual problem in fitted black slacks! Run, Father Titus, run!"

Ah! But which way? By what system of conscience shall he aim himself? Must he run from the peril of sin by only the *safer* course and thus declare himself a Tutiorist? No. That is condemned by the church as Rigorism.

Poor flesh and blood seldom get anything but a choice between two unsafe courses. He may, therefore, be an Antitutiorist.

But then, between the less safe courses open to him, must he choose the one that seems more probable not to lead to sin? Or may he go either way, provided the probabilities are equal? If at first, he is a Probabiliorist; if the second, an Equiprobabilist. Or may he have freer choice still and take even the less safe course, so long as there is at least one solidly probable reason to think that good may come of it? In which case, he has opted, along with McHugh, Callan and most of the other casuistical deckhands on the Ark of Salvation, for Probabilism.

He may not, however, do just anything he damn well pleases: That is Laxism, and a very large no-no.

"Oh, see! See Father Titus read the two volumes! See his eyelids droop at Section Six-eighty! See him fall asleep until it's too late to do anything about anything!"

It was all fun, if you liked operating a logic-chopper, but it doesn't thrill me much anymore. For myself, I have more or less parted company with McHugh and Callan and taken up with Norman Mailer. With reservations, of course. My Moral System, at least as worked out to that point, consisted of two propositions: *If it feels right, it is right*; provided everyone intimately and immediately involved has the stomach for it (admittedly, a king-sized *provided*); and *Don't worry excessively about the spiritual danger of getting something for nothing*: There is no such thing as a free lunch. The price of every item on the menu is the same for everybody, good or bad: one crucifixion. No credit cards accepted. Pay the waiter.

So I called her.

Once on Thursday and twice on Friday.

No answer.

Even catching up with Norman Mailer can make you oversleep.

XI

Wednesday, May 16th

While rewriting sexual morality in my head, however, I was also busy with a yellow legal pad, trying to doodle some of the imbalances out of my eschatology. The glory—or the curse—of being human is that you find the former exercise inevitable; the peculiarity of being a dogmatic theologian is that you find the latter just as unavoidable. And even just as salty, sometimes. You catch yourself thinking of subjects like: The Theological Implications of Sex after Death. Profound absurdities. Or absurd profundities. You never know. The only rule is: Juggle the dogmatic images anyway you like; just don't try to work with less than a full set.

Having thus spent the morning scribbling theology and not answering the mail, I decided to spend the afternoon not correcting exam papers. I went over to Audrey Gottschalk's, yellow sheet in hand, to see what she thought of the new set of wings I had dreamt up for my theological coke bottle. Audrey is the parishioner with the correctly fastened head who picked up the flaws in the first design at the coffee hour.

Large rambling house. Odd lots of teenagers lolling about all the time, even when school is in session. Always coffee on the stove; but mercifully, always a half-gallon of California something in the ice box. She and I have had a conversation going for years. About everything in particular. All washed down with what by now must be a river of Chablis. It beats grading papers.

I gave the open door two purely ceremonial knuckle-taps as I wandered into the kitchen.

"Anybody home?"

The Port Jeff Junior High girl math wonder came tearing into the room, chased by her younger brother (grade school, basketball).

"Hi Mary. John. What are you two doing home?"

"John's sick today."

"I hope it's not anything catching. In my weakened condition, I couldn't afford to get that active. Too bad you've got it too."

"No I just figured that if he could stay home, so could I. It's too out nice to sit in that prison."

Smart, free spirit.

"Your mother around?"

"She's here somewhere."

"Do you think you might be able to triangulate, or something, and get a fix on her?"

"Sure."

Out. Like two shots."

By and by, Audrey.

"Hi."

"Good afternoon, Madam. I am visiting the sick, and I thought I would drop by to dispense a little consolation at Port Jefferson's most notable *Krankenhaus*."

In the time it took to say that, she walked straight from the doorway to the dish closet. Two Sau-sea shrimp cocktail glasses, fingers inside. Next stop, ice box: Almadén Rhine. Over to the table, plunked down, poured. She sat.

"Have a seat. What have you been up to?"

"Aside from worrying about your health? I have been solving the theological problems of the world. Or at least, the problems caused by my most recent attempt at solving them. I think I have my finger on the trouble."

"Let's hear it. I'll let you know."

"Well, remember Sunday? You said I had taken away the old imagery but hadn't supplied anything new in its place? That was right, but you could have gone further. I really didn't even get rid of the old imagery. I just came up with an altered version of it.

"How do you mean? It sounded pretty radical to me. No souls. No life after death. No resurrection at the last day. And damn little consolation to boot."

"No, the consolation is there. It's the imagery that's still in the way. Look. In the old imagery, all this stuff was laid out on a horizontal line. You set it out in sequence: First Death, then Resurrection, then Judgment, then

Heaven and Hell. The Mystery worked all along that line; but the fullness of it came only at the end of time—beyond history, *out there*.

"But that's no good. Because the whole point is that the fullness of the Mystery is already one hundred percent present all through history. My mistake was to try to get across the reality of that by saying that since everything is all at once in God—and since God holds us right now in his eternity—it's all really present and accomplished right now in God, even though we can't see it in time."

"All right. That's just the problem. What's your solution?"

"Well, the trouble with saying it that way is that, for all practical purposes, you leave people with the impression that the only place where it's all real is up there in God. And 'up there' is no improvement over 'out there,' when you really come down to it. The mischief is caused, not by the 'up' or the 'out,' but by the 'there.' You can't give the mind two *places* in which to imagine the Mystery at work. Because one of the places is always *here*: It's *this* place, this life, this history. And this world is such an obviously unreconciled mess, that the minute you give them some other place which they can conceive of as unmessy, some nice neat 'there' which is not the untidy 'here,' like the Last Day or the Eternity of God—the minute you do that, a drain in their minds opens and the operative power of the Mystery gets sucked out of the 'here' into the 'there.'"

She pursed her lips for a few seconds, then refilled the glasses.

"How do you get around using two places, though?"

"You reverse the imagery. You have to do that before you can see it right. You don't say, 'My life is hid with Christ in God.' That's true enough, but the 'up there/down there' temptation is too strong to resist. Instead, you say, '*Christ is hidden in my life here.*' And therefore, since he's God, you've got it all right here—without ever having to bring in a 'there' at all.

"As a matter of fact, I think you should probably never think of God as 'there'—at least not in the sense of being somewhere else. Since he is equally and totally present to everything, the only thing that really makes sense is just to say that he's *here*. You can say he's transcendentally here, or immensely here, or omnipresently here, or any-other-fancy-way-you-like here, if you want to get all that in. But you absolutely have to swear off saying he's 'there.'"

"You're going to have a hard time selling that. What about all the 'there' language in the Bible? Are you just going to forget it? What about the Ascension? What about Christ coming back at the end of the world? That's a lot of going and coming. Here to there and back."

"No. I have no intention of getting rid of anything. You don't need to. All you need to do is to know how to handle it. The Ascension is not a literal trip to heaven up above the clouds; it's a historical trip up *as far as the clouds*, used to sacramentalize Christ's exaltation as the Great High Priest. The here/there language isn't meant to tell you where he went; it's meant to tell you what he's like, or how he operates. And when you get it that far, it all begins to click. For instance. He ascends 'up far above all heavens….' That's real 'up there' language, right? But do you know the rest of the line? It's '…that he might fill all things.' And that's strictly 'here' talk. He pours himself into here. The only where he really is, is here. My life is hid with Christ in God, precisely because God in Christ is hidden in my life here. Q.E.D. Back to start. Pretty good, huh?"

"Well, it still doesn't solve the problem of why it's so bad here. That's the real mystery. Maybe you're just fencing with words."

"Maybe. But I go by the clicks. You're never going to get the Mystery down pat anyway. But the clicks at least give you a hint that it's working. Let me read you my morning's output of deathless prose."

She sighed. "I knew it would come to that. Let me find my cigarettes."

I unfolded the paper and waited for her to land and light up.

"Okay. This is where you go once you're locked into the imagery of God *here*:

"'God is intimate to creation. He didn't make it once and walk away; he makes it now and hangs around. Furthermore, he is always busy making: not just the new things, but the old things, too—making good, making up, making over, making love, making out. God's perpetual act of intercourse with creation.

"'And that clicks, because it lands you gracefully back in Scripture. The Bible gives you a God who becomes incarnate, who is eternally and inseparably joined to man and to all the rest of creation, in Jesus. But that incarnation cannot be taken as applying only to Jesus, as if he were God's single, freaky exception to a general policy of keeping his distance from creation; it has got to be the final, grand, clear demonstration of an unvarying policy of being perpetually inside creation. Creation is not a pile of artifacts he has stored in his basement; it's the beloved he's eternally been romancing since Adam and Eve lost Eden.'

"'Which clicks again: because the Lamb slain from the foundation of the world ends up marrying the New Jerusalem prepared as the bride adorned for her husband. *He resides in her forever:* the Endless, Flawless Love Affair as final truth.'"

"Mmh! If that's next Sunday's sermon, I want to sit where I can get a good look at some faces I can think of."

"Let me finish. This was written with you in mind, Love. The theology, I mean:

"'And that, Audrey, you will have to admit, is finally something better than getting philosophical. That is dogmatics as she is done. You don't start out by learning a combination and then just walk in and open the vault. You handle your material with all the fingers you have, and listen for the clicks. Safecracking made as exciting as sex. And vice versa, too—for one last click—but only if you're seriously trying to open up something precious and not just playing around with the knobs.' How's that?"

"Terrible. You get worse every year. You're having a middle-age identity crisis."

AUDREY'S MARRIED DAUGHTER came in with the two bags of groceries.

"Hi, Father. How are you? Mom, you owe me twenty-two-fifty. And that's without the artichokes. I couldn't find them anywhere."

"At those prices, I'm lucky you didn't. But thanks for going shopping for me. Your brother still isn't back with the car."

I had married Francie and her husband a year ago, but hadn't seen her for a while. The conversation rambled from prices, to Washington, to Watergate, to Sam Ervin, to morality in politics, to morality in general, to the morality of living together before you're married in particular, and finally, to the conclusion by all concerned (now, at four, we were five: Michael having finally brought the car back, and Audrey's mother having turned up) that it probably did more good than harm because, if they married, the only thing they were doing new was marrying, and it gave them at least a chance to think about what that might be all about.

Such are the consolations of Audrey's. And you know? When I think of all the drudges condemned from nine to five to making an honest living, I don't feel the least bit guilty. I only wish I could spring them all. The economy would collapse, of course; but it's doing that anyway without my help. At least the winegrowers would get rich. Heaven is a long afternoon.

We broke up. Audrey took three Irish steps of decency with me to the door.

"See you soon."

"Thanks for the warning."

I drove home, shuffled the papers on my desk into three piles, looked at the cartoons in the *New Yorker*, and quit work at four-thirty. Time for *skål*. Elizabeth was throwing together spaghetti alla Matriciana for supper: olive oil, bacon, garlic, tomatoes. She does nice work.

Gin on the rocks with a twist for her.

Gallo Rhine Garten straight for me.

We make each other's drinks.

Such are the consolations of home.

XII

Sunday, May 20th

I SPENT THE rest of the week catching up on my sins of omission: exam papers, mail, Peter Anderson and the rest. On the theological front, my here/there exercise when into the Saturday lecture, and, as usual, came out in Sunday's sermon—slightly laundered, of course. On her way out of the church after mass, Audrey said one word: "Coward!"

During the hymn before mass, however, I looked around for the wide-brimmed straw hat. No sign, until the middle of the third stanza. Then, behind two tall men, a glimpse of it in the right rear pew. Because of the six-footers, however, and the way she held her head low, I didn't get much of a look at her until afterward. Even if I could have, though, I wouldn't have looked at her during the sermon.

I've never quite figured it out, but there is a logic to

the way I decide which faces to watch while preaching. Part of it is picking out the animated ones, of course. You want a standard by which you can judge whether you're making sense; so you talk to the fellow halfway back who frowns when you're explaining something, and you keep explaining till you get the frown off his face. If you can find someone who unconsciously nods when he catches on, even better.

But there's more to it than that. I find I never watch any faces I really know, or want to know. I never watch my wife, for example, or my secretary, or Audrey. Nor in this case, did I watch Pat Donahue. Why? Too close for comfort, maybe? Too many items on those agendas which might interfere with a single-minded effort to get something said? Avoidance of perceptive critics? I don't know. You tell me.

In any case, she was the last one out at the end of mass. I almost thought she had left early again and I hadn't seen her. Slight qualms. But this time, not based on concern over the effects of sermons. Not based on anything admitted. Just plain, keep-looking-over-the-shoulder-of-the-one-you're-shaking-hands-with-now qualms. Then, finally.

"Nice to see you again. How've you been?"

"Fine, thank you."

"I saw you last week, but you escaped early."

"I know. I left right after communion. I was taking my children up to my mother's in Massachusetts for a week and I wanted to leave in time to get there for supper."

"Did you spend the week, too?"

"Yes, it'd been a long while since I spent any time with her. I enjoyed it. It was a good idea."

The heart snatches at explanations even faster than the mind. Big sense of relief caused by a running broad jump to the conclusion that her absence hadn't meant she was trying to avoid me, and that therefore I wasn't out of the game. Some consternation, however, at having to admit for the first time that I was in it.

"Well, it's great to see you. Any time."

"I'm sorry if I was rude when I left your office that day. All of a sudden, I was afraid I'd said too much. Driving home, I just felt drained. But it did do me good to say it all out loud: I don't think I would have thought of taking the trip if I hadn't talked to you."

"Well, good. As I said, any time."

"I would really like that. But you've got to be busy."

"Nonsense. Listen. Tuesday's free. Would you like to come then?"

"Well, if it really isn't too much trouble…"

"Of course not. How about the same time?"

"All right, Tuesday at one. Thanks."

"See you then."

What game?

XIII

Tuesday, May 22nd

I WAS ON the phone in the back hall when she arrived, so my secretary showed her into the office. When I got there, I pulled a side chair over to the couch. General Pastoral Rule No. 534: There is nothing harder than talking to a priest, unless it's talking to a priest sitting in a swivel chair behind a desk.

"How's everything going?"

"Better, really. Not all the time, but at least now and then. Which is more than I could say before."

"Talking is a funny thing. People come to priests or psychiatrists or whatever, thinking that they'll find someone who can tell them how to set things right. But that seldom happens. Partly because the priest doesn't very often know what to say; and partly because, even if he does, they hardly ever take the advice. But mostly because, in really big difficulties, there is very little that can be done anyway. So it boils down to listening a lot while the person talks himself through to his own kind of wisdom or relief. After you left, I thought over the conversation. I told you practically nothing. I did think of a couple of things to say, but it just didn't seem the right time to say them."

"I'm sorry I talked so much. It just seemed to pour out."

"That's inevitable. You'd been sitting on the whole business for years. But at least, while Ted was alive, you had someone to talk to about it. Even the hassles were probably a kind of relief. But after he died, the unmentionable subject became really unmentionable anywhere. In that situation, nothing gets better until you can find some place to talk it out where you're sure it will stay unmentioned. Which is what priests are for."

Her eyes narrowed almost imperceptibly. She was sitting with her legs crossed. Her hands, which had been resting on her knees, were suddenly pulled back to her lap. She held her forearms.

"I didn't think it was unmentionable. What we had was beautiful. It's just that it couldn't be talked about because of other people."

Damn! When you're a priest, you keep forgetting that other people never forget it. They expect a judgmental attitude, and unless you weigh every word, they hear what they expect. Time to back up and regroup:

"It was a bad word. Sorry. I only meant what you said."

She shook off the apology with a toss of her head.

"Still, that attitude is always there. The idea that it's the other people who were right, and we were the ones who were wrong. I felt it most of the time. Not in myself, but through Ted. Which is just as bad, when you love somebody."

(I have a habit. When it comes time to have a man-to-man, let's-stop-the-nonsense talk with myself, I assume the role of my alter ego and address myself as Arthur.

(I said, Look, Arthur. You're not going to be able to fake your way out of this misunderstanding by talking at a distance from yourself. She wants to know, Who is that masked man? Cut the Lone Ranger act.)

"All right," I said. "Let's get that one off the board first. I didn't mean to bring it up, but that doesn't make any difference: It's up. The question in plain English, is, What do I think about adultery? And my answer is, I just don't know any more. Adultery is such a complicated notion, I can't deal with it on a simple right-or-wrong basis. For instance, if it means infringing on some other guy's exclusive right to everything about his wife, I can't decide, because I think that kind of exclusivity in personal relationships is just a five-thousand-year-old red herring which smells more like the work of the devil than God. At least, where it's taken seriously, it produces situations which look more like hell than heaven.

"But if it means just random screwing around, I come down on the side that says it's wrong. I think that trivializes sex. And since nothing human beings do is ever really trivial—it's all dynamite, even scratching somebody's back—it's just moronic to say that sex is nothing but glorified backscratching.

"But then again, if it means that falling in love, as such, is sinful, or that you have to draw a bunch of dumb lines across every love affair—like, you can talk but not touch, or touch but not kiss, or kiss but not hug, and so on down to bed—I think that's all crazy. People just do fall in love. I can see a moral obligation for two people to be careful for each other, and to be careful for the sake of other people who think differently from the way they do—who can't live without drawing all those lines for them—but I can't see any necessity for them to think they ought to draw such lines themselves.

"I guess where I'm at is accepting, in some sense, the church's insistence that adultery is wrong, but thinking that the notion is so fouled up that a lot of things normally classified as adultery could, in some circumstances, be right. Which, maybe, is what you were saying about it's being beautiful and not feeling in yourself that it was wrong."

She let go of her arms and lit a cigarette.

"I guess so. It's funny though, how you can be so sure—really sure—that it's good, and still go on feeling wrong."

I unwrapped a Marsh Wheeling, bit the end off, and took my time lighting it.

"I know. It's hard to figure what that's about. Maybe it's just a hangover from the bad old days when the label on the bottle said sex was nasty. We're not drinking that stuff any more, but we've still got to get through the morning after. But then again, maybe it's a sign that sex is one of the really big mysteries and we ought to be very careful about putting it in simplistic little cans labeled right and wrong. In any case, however, thank you Ma'am for helping me with my pastoral problem. You're a good listener. When may I make another appointment?"

She smiled. "Any time."

"Good. Fins then."

She crossed two fingers and help them up.

"Fins."

At last. A way out of The Subject.

"You must be from Queens."

"How did you know?"

"Only kids from Queens know what 'fins' means. Other places, they call it Pax or Kings-X."

"I thought everybody said 'fins.' But you're right: I was born in Astoria.

"Whereabouts?"

"We lived on Forty-third Street between Jamaica and Grand."

"That's fascinating. My wife comes from around the block: Forty-fourth Street. Did you know a family named Clark?"

"No. but I only lived there till I was ten. After that, we moved to Mineola, which is where I was till I moved out here. My husband and I were married at Holy Nativity."

"How big was your family?"

"I was an only child. Spoiled rotten."

"You've got company. I grew up in Jackson Heights and I was also an only child. My parents bent over backward to be strict, but I fooled them. I ended up spoiled rotten anyway."

I spotted the opening.

"Listen. I've got an idea. Stop me if I'm wrong, but, even though it may not be easy, you really do want to talk about Ted. Well, from a different point of view, so do I. Remember the first day you came here, I said I had been thrown together with him quite a lot, but that I was never really close to him? I think I said we were two different breeds of cat."

She nodded, but said nothing.

"Well, that bothers me now. What I was really doing with him all those years was the same spoiled-brat trick I pull on lots of people: take only as much of them as you find convenient and duck the rest. But that's bad news, because what is really means is that you're not taking *them* at all. It makes for a comfortable life, and if you learn to be humorous about it, you hardly ever have to be nasty. But it's a cop-out. You don't get annoyed only because you don't get involved. People just can't get near you.

"But the sad part about that is, you don't get near them either, and your life ends up narrower because of it. In the end, if you never changed, you'd be nothing but the sum of your own prejudices.

"What I'm saying, I suppose, is that I feel guilty now as far as he's concerned. Not only because if I'd been closer to him, maybe, the pressure on him could have been shared. That's possible, but not likely. You were closer to him than I would ever have been, and it all happened anyway. It's just that I feel as if I'd thrown away something I should have known more about, and that now, while I can't get him back as he was, I might at least get to know him a little better through you."

"Is that what you meant when you said it's not just a one-way street?"

"I didn't have that in mind then, but it's certainly one of the meanings."

"That's good. When you said it, I just thought you were being polite about me taking up your time. I didn't think there was any way it could really matter to you."

She caught herself.

"I didn't mean that the way it sounded. I know that as a priest it matters to you because it's somebody's problem. But I didn't think that as a person it would."

"Look. Let's put 'fins' on that priest/person business, too. When in doubt, think person. Priesting is something a person does, not something he disappears into. Me William, you Patricia. Two-way street."

"Okay, but make it Pat."

"And Bill. And no more apologies."

WE TALKED FOR about an hour and a half. I could see why Ted liked more than her looks. She was not a high-powered thinker, but she was very seldom wrong when she finally worked something through. And she had a memory like flypaper. Or, better yet, like an old bureau drawer. Everything, needed or not, went into it. It could be closed up and left untouched for as long as she liked, but her experiences were all still in there, waiting to be picked over, sorted and, eventually, even understood. My mind holds onto facts only if it can build a framework for them. Hers had an apparently limitless capacity for unclassified detail.

She remembered, for example, a great deal more than I did about the first sermon she heard me preach. When I go on one of my theological benders, all I really hold in my mind is the line, the thread of the argument. If the binge lasts long enough I sometimes end up repeating myself badly, since I either don't recall where or to whom I mentioned a particular detail, or else I forget it completely and think I'm inventing it from scratch. (After two months of Sundays on death and resurrection, Audrey asked me how much longer I thought my seizure would last: I had been using the same illustration of the way God holds creation for eight weeks.)

The interesting thing about Pat was that, while she had tucked away all the points about not needing to talk about souls, or about life after death, she didn't have any particular problems with them. It was over her head, she said. Most people have to forget before they can overlook things. She could remember something and skip it at the same time. That didn't apply quite so much when either her mind or her emotions genuinely caught on; but even so, her ability to hold contradictories in the unbothered state was positively enviable. Ted must have found her an oasis.

We fall in love, not only with bodies, but with turns of mind, quirks of imagination. As a matter of fact, it is precisely the sudden, admiring perception of those turns that is the rising wave which catches us from behind and hurls us out of infatuation into romance. The metaphysical validation of desire. It's either the greatest thing in the world or the cruelest trick of all. Or both, most likely. But it's as irresistible as the rollers of the sea.

Talking to her, I could almost feel what it must have been like when he was first caught up by it. The long physical attraction—a year, she said. Growing, casual intimacy: shaking hands; long goodbyes holding hands; his hand on her upper arm; his arm lightly around her waist; her arm around his for the first time; the tacit squeeze at the door. All great, all fun. And all as manageable as breathing. Even if it lands them right in bed after the first hug. Make it the greatest lust in the world: It still is nothing compared to the all-legitimating, all-blinding onrush of admiration.

There he was, in his life of perpetual bother, where no concern was ever less than total, and the day without an agony of contradiction never came. And there she sat, in a quiet house on a sunny afternoon, unrattled, open, at ease, and strong. She said she thought his love grew underneath and broke through only when he first kissed her. I don't think that's right. I'd be willing to bet that, for at least a while before that, he knew he was in love with her. The wave of admiration had already caught him far out in the surf, and there was no mistaking that it would carry him all the way in. The only thing his lust did was take away his fear of it for a while.

And when they lay together afterward in the delicious emptiness of the pleasure-spent, it finally beached him for good: *She* was marvelous. *She* was his peace. He wanted to lie forever in the shade of her serenity, to rest his head on the arm of her strength: *O God! I love you, I love you.*

After that, of course, fear again. But, by then, too late.

XIV

Tuesday, May 22nd

AT ANY RATE, she and I talked about Ted. There was an immediacy about her which, coupled with the welter of detail she kept pulling out of her memory, gave the impression that somehow Ted was present in her, and therefore present to me. It's tempting to write that kind of thing off as illusion, but I'm not so sure. At the very least, it provides some imagery to back up my notion that you don't need to think about the dead in terms of life after death, only in terms of their literal, mortal lives, held somehow in an eternal way.

For example. The six years of her affair with Ted were present in the world in a number of different ways. First, historically, literally, successively, as all events in time are: coming into being and passing away, moving from past to future on the point of the second hand, balanced on an unstoppable, knife-edged 'now.' (Which, incidentally, is the old Latin definition of time: *nunc volans*, 'now' flying.) But those same six years are also present to her now, all at once, at least in memory. The fleeting, successive 'nows' of the past stand all together in her mind in a kind of eternity. (Which, nicely enough again, is the old Latin definition of eternity: *nunc stans*, 'now' standing still.)

These two modes of presence are, of course, not the same thing. But they might well both be images of the same thing. As a matter of fact, the real theological insight is probably that both those presences—the affair as held successively in history and the affair as held all at once in memory—are images of the Mystery by which it is held in its fullness in God.

Because, if you use them as images, you begin to get somewhere. The clicks again. The strength of the successive, historical image, for example, is its solidity: it suggests unquestionable reality, not some shadowy stand-in for reality. But it has its limitations. It suggests that a person's past and future are really inaccessible to him—that only the pinpoint of the 'now' is really real. Which is nonsense. Because my past is present to me now, not only in memory, but in fact: the hangover from last night's Scotch and bridge till four A.M., the hangup about high heels from God knows where, and the ability to hang-in which I caught, or inherited, from my father. And my future is present to me now, too. Not as a dim unknown, but as the bright, known hope which is the main engine of my humanity. Admittedly, my knowledge of it may frequently be wrong, but that's only incidental: Right or wrong, it remains the motor that drives me.

And that's where the image of the affair as held in memory has the advantage. It may lack the solidity of the historical image, but it thumps hard for the real presence, all at once, of past, present, and future. Those six successive years—that inching accumulation of the past in the hope of a future—all of it is now in her mind. Better yet, the interrelations of it all can be seen in memory as they cannot be seen in history. In memory, if she wishes, she can start with the future first, and go back over it all in any direction she likes. She is not limited to fingering her way forward along a single, straight string; she is free to explore the whole as the web it really is. Which makes marvelous sense, because now there is at last no doubt about the future which was the engine that drove their lives. The results have yet to be assessed; but all the counties have finally been heard from, beginning with the midwife's slap on the bottom, and ending with the abutment at Exit 36: Let the hunt for meaning now begin!

Maybe that's the best image of what God does with our lives: Just as we hold the web of them in memory, he holds the web of them in Christ. When Christ appears in our deaths, there we are complete in him, ready at last to start the exploration we spent our lives mostly just packing for. You can take a few excursions into it before that, but the limitations are so crippling that the real trip has to wait for the end: "In my end is my beginning."

So you've got three images of the holding: The affair as held in history, the affair as held in memory, and the affair as held in Christ. The first is more real but less free, the second less real but nicely unfettered; and the third, if it's true, has the advantages of both and the drawbacks of neither. But just for good measure, I'll give you one more.

Their affair is present now, really and operatively, *in my life*. Simply because it is operative and real in her, and she is operative and real to me. The whole tissue of it is held, not only in her memory, but in *her*—in her body, her intellect, her emotions—in her *person* sitting now in my office. That's why I'm slow to write off the impression of Ted's presence in her as an illusion produced by some kind of unconscious conjuring on her part. The conjuring may be there all right, but what it produces may still be real: "Imaginary gardens with real toads in them." We are complex, and we hold each other in webs of incredible intricacy. I don't want to reduce the image of the holding to some one-lung operation like memory. After all, she held him many ways while he was alive. Held him up, held him to her, held him in her. She was a vessel for holding him then; why can't she be one now?

For if Christ, the holder of all, is in her, then all he holds is in her, too. And by that one fact, all our images of the holding become more than images. If his indwelling is real, every one of them becomes a sacrament, a real presence, a communication of beings, a Communion of Saints—a holding of the Mystery of his Holding, by which all men are borne into the opening out of the web.

I walked her to the end of the path at the edge of the parking lot and watched her go across to her car. Besides having a fascinating memory, she had a memorable walk. She was wearing a white blouse and a short, tight blue skirt, bare legs. Open brown leather sandals. All very, very easy to watch, especially her legs. But it was the walk that was spectacular. It was just one eighth of an inch this side of a wiggle. Back in the days of three-inch spike heels, it must have stopped traffic.

My wife drove in while she was walking to her car. I gave her a kiss, hauled three bags of groceries out of the back seat and tramped back up the path to the rectory with her.

"Thanks. I would have died lugging those."

"No problem. Just open the door for me."

"Who was that?"

"Her name is Patricia Donahue. She's from Coram."

"St. Aidan's?"

"She's gone there, but she's also been here at the ten-thirty a couple of times. She lives in Strathmore East."

"She has a walk and a half on her."

"You said it. It would take a brave man to squire that into *La Côte Basque*."

XV

Tuesday, May 22nd

I put the groceries down on the kitchen counter. "What's in the ice box that's cold, wet and light?"

"You have a choice. There's left-over iced tea from last night and half a bottle of flat ginger ale. Your children drank all the beer and soda."

"That's a choice?"

"That's it, unless you want something harder on the rocks."

"Later. Care to join me in a dead ginger ale?"

"No thank you."

I poured my own. Elizabeth is consummately accurate. The bottle is precisely half full, and no smallest bubble mars its flawless flatness. My oldest children and their army of friends are passing through their Bourbon and ginger ale phase at the expense of my Jack Daniel's and Canada Dry's carbonation. They are better at removing bottle caps than replacing them. I make a wish that they will be given repentance, better minds, and a preference for Scotch and tap water. The office phone rings.

It's a woman I don't know. Can I marry her daughter this Saturday? No, I am in Garden City all day every Saturday. Sorry. Do I know of anybody who could? Possibly, but she would have to call them herself. I suggest the Presbyterian and Methodist ministers. Do I have their phone numbers? Yes. Hold on. Thank you. Goodbye. They probably won't do it either.

Short-order weddings. I hate them. Mercifully, the Episcopal Church has finally put a thirty-day notification requirement in the marriage canon, to allow for at least an attempt at decent premarital counseling. What goes on is simply appalling: People come to you to make the biggest formal commitment in their lives, and they approach it with less thought than they'd give to buying an old jar at a yard sale. They don't even phone the priest themselves. They let Mama do it. Maybe the church ought to get out of the wedding business altogether. The marriage-salvage business would be quite enough to keep us busy.

Footsteps on the porch. I look out the window. Anne Jacobs! Unbelievable. First Pat. Then a five-minute interlude with flat ginger ale and Liz's curiosity about Pat. Then Anne. Sometimes I think I live under the original monstrous regiment of women. It's not all bad, of course, but the guardian angels are cutting the timing awfully close.

"Anne! How are you?"

"Am I interrupting anything?"

"No. Come on in. I'm as free as the wind. What brings you up this way?"

"I'm looking for a wedding present for my brother's daughter and I thought I'd try the 1812 House."

"Liz has had good luck down there. They have a glass-and-silver martini pitcher with a stirrer for under twenty dollars. At the price, it's really quite nice."

"I'll look for it. The reason I dropped by is to see if you could give me the names of the real estate contacts you mentioned. I've done a little looking on the South Shore, but I still want to check things out up here."

She sat. I copied the names and phone numbers on an index card for her. Not only were the angels cutting the timing close; they were slicing the spaces paper-thin. All I needed was to have Pat and Anne wind up in this parish. Short prayer to Richard Cardinal Cushing, patron saint of real estate, to live up to his reputation for shrewdness and keep me off the hook.

"How are things going for you?"

"Pretty well. It isn't easy; but everyone has been so kind. That doesn't help with the loneliness when it's acute, of course, or with the blank wall I come up against when I try to understand it; but I'm lucky in having the friends I do."

Rapid-fire series of questions through my mind. She's normally hard to read, but today she seems a little more open. Does she want to talk? Should I just wait and make conversation? Or should I raise the question myself? If so, which question? Ted in general? Ted just before his death? The note? Her conclusions, if any? Maybe the last. Just don't unleash the curiosity.

"I suppose, even with all the information in the world, nobody's understanding is up to the job. We're all such mysteries, even to ourselves. Still though, we go right on craving explanations. Maybe it just proved what Chesterton said about mystery being the mind's real home."

"You're right. It's not that I'm lacking information. I have more than I can deal with, really, but none of it harmonizes. Ted had been restless and nervous for a long time. He even talked about its being time to move on to another parish. I thought he was just pushing himself too hard. He would make calls all day, and then go out at least two nights a week and make even more. And that's without counting the meetings most of the rest of the nights. He would come in around eleven, fall asleep watching the news, go to bed dead tired, and then lie awake half the night. We hadn't had much of a home life for quite a while."

The temptation to jump to conclusions is almost overwhelming, especially when what's going into the left ear bumps into what went into the right an hour ago. But it's still useless: Just sit tight.

"Sounds as if the pressure was getting to him. Do you think he was consciously aware of it? I mean, did he ever admit it or seem to want help with it?"

"No. If I brought it up, he would insist there was no problem. And if I ever went so far as to suggest that he take some time off, he'd get testy and even more withdrawn than usual. I wanted to ask him to go to some kind of counselor, but I couldn't seem to get the word 'counseling' out of my mouth for fear of driving him further away. I had all kinds of conversations with him in my mind in which I would think of gentle ways to suggest seeing a psychiatrist, but that word was even more impossible to get out than 'counseling.' Maybe I shouldn't have been so reserved, but I just didn't have the nerve for anything else. I guess I was actually handling myself with kid gloves even more than I was him."

"Listen. We all do that. Sparing ourselves under the guise of sparing others. You're pretty strong to be able to admit it. Most of us never do. But the important thing to remember is that even if you were dead-right in your self-blame, it's still supremely important never to let yourself get into the blaming business. Because it takes your mind off the one thing that matters. The main thing to be dwelt on is the reconciliation of everything and everybody in Christ. All the mistakes, all the failures, all the shortfalls, and all the foul-ups—inside us and outside us—have somehow been set right by his death. Reconciliation is a mystery the mind can find a home in. Blame is just an unsolvable puzzle that drives you out of your head."

She thought for a few seconds. Hard to tell which way she was going. One, unvarying, pleasant face. No body language.

"Still, though, you go right on feeling guilty. It's like a tooth that hurts: You keep poking at it even when it doesn't bother you, just so you can feel the pain again."

"It's a good analogy, but it doesn't quite fit. You touch the tooth in the hope that this time it won't hurt. That's more or less natural. Messing around with blame is like sipping poison. The real point is that God isn't blaming anybody. All the blame has been soaked up into the death of Christ: out of the world into the Giant Eternal Blotter. We're all forgiven everything. You, me, Ted, everybody. That's the Good News. The only bad news is our insisting that somehow we're not. I don't know why it's so hard for us to get that straight, but it is. The church has an absolutely rotten record of getting itself to take the biggest promise of Christ seriously."

Good Lord, Arthur, is that ever true! All those centuries of sin-sheets. All that endless fuss in confession about exactly how blameworthy this act or that thought is. "… especially, I accuse myself of the following sins: boasting three times, and maybe once talking about myself when I didn't have to; and masturbation twice, but only alone, not with others." Oh sure, there were warnings about the dangers of scrupulosity, but they were really just salve the church spread on her own conscience for all the damage she did by tarring everybody with the blame brush. The majority of the race, of course, were tough enough bastards not to take it too seriously; but the poor, sensitive souls, who were already half-bonkers anyway, took it all in and got really freaked out. Either way, however, it turned what should have been a celebration of forgiveness into an orgy of guilt and stood the gospel right smack on its head.

She went back to the tooth, though.

"I know. But you still keep trying to solve the puzzle. I told you he always resented my suggesting he take time off. There was one exception. The Monday and Tuesday before he died, he went over to the Friary and spent the night. It wasn't a scheduled retreat. He just said he was going to relax and think."

Another false lead. For her, and probably for Ted, too. More damned bookkeeping. Relax? Great idea. Lean back in the Everlasting Arms. You're being hugged and kissed to death by the greatest lover of all. He's got it all together. Nothing you've ever done or will do amounts to a hill of beans compared to the Holy Mountain of Reconciliation.

But think? Terrible. Because that almost always means fussing over the books. What did he do over there at the Friary? Did he go to confession? If so, did some confessor screw him up with a lecture on the evils of adultery? Or did he screw himself up without outside help? Did he decide to drop Pat, and then find he couldn't? Or did he decide to leave Anne and realize he couldn't do that either? And then what? Did he decide that because he couldn't live with two sets of books, he had to kill the bookkeeper? If so, who did he think told him two sets of books were the sin against the Holy Ghost? Not God, Arthur. Some mother of a church maybe, or some other mother but not God. Peter kept two sets of books. And Paul, too, probably. And Judas, for sure. The difference was that Peter and Paul managed somehow to remember that God doesn't give a damn whether you or I can pass an audit. He's already blotted out the handwriting that was against us. But Judas forgot that. He had to get it all together himself; and, in the effort, all he did was knock himself apart. We've all got one shining purpose and two sets of books. And most of us, one way or another, get tripped up by it, because this is a bitchy, unforgiving world. But if God says it doesn't matter—if he takes in prodigals, and pays everybody equally at the end—where in hell do we get off deciding that there are some performances he's got to hold against us?

The sheer, point-missing genius of it all! The surpassing ability to hit the bull's-eye on the wrong target! The offer of free grace duly received; but then expounded as meaning that there's nothing good you can do to earn your way in, instead of that there's nothing bad you can do to keep yourself out.

I tried one corner of that on her.

"The trouble is, that when most of us start thinking, we imagine we're under some solemn necessity to come up with answers that will make us more acceptable to God. God only knows what was bothering Ted. But it doesn't matter. The real point is that God has said once for all on the cross that, whatever it was, it isn't bothering God. Even if we can't get it all together, he can, and he will, and he has, and he does.

"Forgive me, but I'm on one of my pet subjects. You know my favorite parable for all this? The king who threw the wedding party for his son. First he invites all his classy friends—all the old money with the right connections and the right manners and the chauffeur-driven Bentleys and the Givenchy gowns. The beautiful people who can really make a gorgeous, gala evening—a reconciled, perfect party.

"Well, they all give him chintzy excuses and beg off. So the king has one tremendous fit, writes them off as a bunch of deadbeats, and decides to make a reconciled party on his own: He sends out his servants and tells them to drag in anybody they can find. So the servants go down to the Bowery and they round up a bunch of numbers runners, old whores, and drunks asleep in doorways with wine bottles in brown paper bags. They even get the grifter down on Christie Street who waits till your car is stopped for a light and then hits you for a dime not to wipe your windshield with a greasy rag. And then they bring this deluxe assortment of bums, tarts and winos to the palace, and the king goes to work on them.

"He phones up the wardrobe mistress at the Royal Opera Company and has her send over all the costumes she can spare. Then he gives everybody a free costume at the door and tells them to go wash up and change. Any costume they like, any one at all.

"Well, the party starts, and it looks gorgeous. The champagne flows, and the hors d'oeuvres never stop coming, and pretty soon some of the gorgeousness begins to rub off on the guests themselves. The drinks are free, so they stop cadging and swiping bags from each other. They catch glimpses of themselves in the mirror, and they're so surprised at how good they look, they actually start acting better. They use manners they thought they'd forgotten years ago.

"And everything goes fine until the king sees this one sourpuss standing next to the door with his costume in a heap at his feet. And he goes over to him and says 'what's wrong? Doesn't it fit? You don't like it? Take another.' But he's grumpy and won't answer. And the king tries again and says, 'Come on, put it on. Join the party.' But he still won't talk. And then the king gets really mad and says, 'Look Buster, this is my party, and I'm not going to have you louse it up for no reason. If you don't like it, you can leave.'

"But the grouch won't leave either, so the king calls the Royal Bouncer and says, 'Marty, you see this punk here? Convince him he can go to hell if he doesn't like my party. And convince him right now.'

"You see? The point is, there is nothing you need to do to get in. You only have to accept the reconciliation which has already been made for you. And above all, there is nothing you can do to keep from getting in. Those servants the king sent—they all carried pistols. The only way you can get out of the party is to refuse the reconciliation—to think that your own moral preoccupations or whatever, are more important than putting on the free costume, and joining the fun.

"Nobody has to do any bookkeeping. Ted's reconciled already. And so are you, and so am I. All we have to do is throw the ledgers in the trash can and get on with the party."

For the first time, she showed a little surprise.

"That doesn't sound particularly moral."

"Exactly. Most of the parables are made deliberately immoral—the elder son gets gypped, the people who worked all day aren't paid more than the ones who worked only an hour—just to make the point that it's the Mystery of reconciliation that's the main thing, not the moral bookkeeping."

"It's so hard to shake the habit, though."

"Sure it is. But it's the most important habit in the world to shake. Because if it's really true that God isn't counting, then bookkeeping is the supreme exercise in unreality. We're already home free. The party is already in full swing. Accept. Enjoy, enjoy."

She smiled a little.

"Well, at least it's worth a try. You make it sound awfully cheerful. Ted used to say he wished he could be as relaxed as you. He never knew quite what to make of you, you know. On the kind of subjects he was interested in, you always struck us as—well, cold. Smart, but a little worldly and cynical. It's nice to hear you get wound up about something. Really nice, I mean. It's a side of you that doesn't show enough."

"Fair enough. That's worth a try on my side. Thank you, Madam, for your solicitousness."

She stood up to go. I took her hand and gave her a peck on the cheek.

"I really mean it. Thanks."

"My pleasure. Thank you."

I think it was the first time in all the years I knew her that she talked *to* me rather than at me. At least it's the first time I remember her dealing with me as a subject. And, probably for just that reason, it was also the first time I realized she actually was capable of making a sexual impression.

Funny, why should that be? What in the world was their sex life all about? For a guess, I'd say slow on her part at the beginning, but growing all the time. A much bigger thing in her life than she ever consciously understood. And on his part, pretty much the reverse: Great for openers, but then fouled up by a guilty conscience over Pat. Maybe next to nothing the last couple of years.

Which was one more thing to get to him. The mistress, who is so sure of her sexuality she can take it or leave it, is the one who winds his clock ten times out of ten. And the wife, who needs it more than either of them knows, gets nothing but a limp dick. To her that hath shall be given, and from her that hath not...

God, what a screwed-up subject! Guilt over the mistress. Then guilt on top of that over not being able to get it up for his wife. He breaks not only the Old Law from Mount Sinai, but also the New Law of the Marriage Manual. And on top of that, when he's dead and gone, it's a relief to his wife, even though she doesn't know it yet.

She's a woman again, not a failure in bed. She hasn't held a clock key in her hand for years, but, by George, she still remembers how to use one, even in the dark. Give her eighteen months and somebody's in for a winding. Wish her well.

But don't ask me who's to blame for all the whacked-up thinking that goes on. I can slice that head cheese from either end. If you want me to, I can blame it on sinful man's transgression of the law of nature forbidding adultery. Or, if you don't like that, I can blame it on the repressions caused by a totally unnecessary poking of the universe's guilt-sniffing nose into something which is nobody's business but that of the two lovers. Both true. Both false, too, I suppose. But in either case, both just two more goose chases after the utterly wrong subject. We are all royally screwed up, and none of us is about the be anything else. Blaming yourself is no better and no worse than excusing yourself. They're both irrelevant. Because the job is beyond either. You couldn't save yourself if you tried, and you don't have to try because he's already done it.

God, it is just so obvious! One Main Subject: RECONCILIATION, ΚΑΤΑΛΛΑΓΗ, RECONCILIATIO. And here we are, three fourths of the way through our twentieth century of talking about everything else but.

XVI

Tuesday, May 22nd

I saw Anne to the door, went back into the office, and put my feet up on the desk.

There's a large sleeper in this business of reconciliation. The king in the parable of the marriage feast gets rid of the nuisance at the end by having the bouncers bind him hand and foot and cast him into outer darkness. Then, presumably, he goes back to the party and just forgets about him.

But that won't wash: God doesn't forget. And not just because he has a long memory and can remember things that once were. He's got more than bad memories to reconcile. He doesn't have just the thoughts of things. He's got the things themselves. Because everything that ever was or will be in this temporal world is held in one, simultaneous, eternal 'now' in God. And it's held there, not only intellectually, but really. God has no idle thoughts. When he thinks something, it jumps out of nothing into being, once and forever. When God the Father thinks *Tyrannosaurus rex*, God the Holy Spirit broods *Tyrannosaurus rex* over the void, and God the Word says *Tyrannosaurus rex* over the brooding. And presto, they Three, in their Undivided Unity, are everlastingly stuck with one ugly lizard.

But do you see what that means? No doubt, there are a great many pleasant creatures in the Land of the Trinity at the Marriage Supper of the Lamb—fuzzy ducklings, gorgeous girls and the spacious firmament rejoicing in reason's ear. But remember, he's got it *all* together. And that means all the pain and all the dying, all the betrayals and all the lies. It means the bastinado and the rack, and hanging, drawing and quartering. It means electric shocks in the genitals and teeth pulled out, one by one, without novocaine. In short, it means all the torture, misery, and inhumanity that creatures have ever dished out to one another. And it means that all of that is perpetually present in God.

And there's the real problem. It bothers us only when it gets too close to us. But it bothers him all the time, because it has nowhere else but him in which to happen. He always knows it because it always is; and it always is because his knowledge is the root cause of it all. *What does he do then with the evil?* How does he get it out of the banquet hall so it doesn't ruin the party?

"I will forgive their iniquity, and I will remember their sin no more."

Great. But how does Omniscience forget? How does

the Brooding Spirit end up without a care in the world? How does the Creating Word shut up?

The outer darkness is no help. "If I go down to hell, thou art there also." There is no outer darkness. If the promise is true, then the reconciliation can occur only by virtue of some inner darkness in God himself. But what could that be?

I put my feet down and scribbled some notes:

1. The death of Christ as eternal.

2. The death of Christ as the eternal cesspool into which the muck is flushed.

3. The outer darkness as inner darkness. The king walking around laughing with his guests after he's eaten all the rot himself.

4. Charles Williams. The sequestering of the knowledge of evil in the Word of God.

5. Christ's eternally dead, utterly blank human mind as the black hole into which the Risen Lord sequesters the sins and iniquities of the world.

6. Christ's forever stilled human tongue as the device by which the eternally garrulous Word manages to unmention the unmentionable.

7. The Silence of the Word.

Liz came in.

"I thought you had somebody here."

"I did, but they left a while ago."

Arthur, Arthur, when are you going to stop that 'they'

trick? Your wife took about one year of marriage to learn to read 'she' every time you use it.

"Well, it's four-thirty. Are you coming out for *skål?* You said you'd talk about Sunday's dinner."

"Be right with you. Hold on, I'll walk you back."

Notes into the drawer.

Stretch.

Civilization.

XVII

Tuesday, May 22nd

Liza had thawed out a dish of *moussaka* from the freezer as well as a couple of *spanakopitas* that were left over after a party, so there was really nothing to do but crank up the oven. We made drinks, and I threw together the makings of a Greek salad just to keep in the spirit of the thing: garlic rubbed in the bowl, lettuce, chicory, scallions, anchovies, feta, Greek olives, orégano, pepper. Salt, oil and vinegar ready on the table. Did she want to open a can of stuffed grape leaves? No, save them. Did she want a little dill in it? No, don't guck it up. We still had fifteen minutes, so we went out and sat on the porch.

"How many are we going to be for dinner Sunday?"

She ticked them off: "Gottschalks [that's Audrey and Bill], Harrises, Larsens and us. If you're game, I thought maybe we'd go Chinese."

"Sure. What time did you tell them?"

"Seven-thirty. There's a thing of lasagne in the freezer I can feed the kids."

"That gives me all afternoon. How many dishes do you want?"

"Five should be enough."

"For eight you should have at least six."

"Keep it simple."

We went around the Chinese barn several times. I told her I would make shrimp toast for an hor d'oeuvre and follow up at dinner with two steamed dishes: pearl balls, and fish slices with ginger and black mushrooms.

"Don't overdo the ginger. Half the time you drown out the flounder."

Next I offered shredded pork and vegetables with oyster sauce, rolled up in thin omelettes; string beans or asparagus, whichever, Szechuan style; beef and celery; and chicken and peanuts.

She observed that I had now hit seven. The Szechuanese beans were vetoed because the kitchen always gets smoked up, and the beef and celery because of lack of interest.

"Okay. How about shrimp and ketchup?"

"You already have a shrimp dish. Keep it at five. This isn't Chinese New Year. The next thing you'll want is two of the kids in a dragon suit. Besides, I would like you at the table some of the time."

I folded.

"All right. What to drink?"

"White wine or beer, whichever they want. I'll have

both unless your children clean me out."

"No Chablis though. Something a little sweeter so it can stand up to the chicken and peanuts."

"The ones who drink wine prefer Chablis, which will go fine with everything else—even with the chicken, if you don't use so much red pepper. Besides, you and Bill Gottschalk always drink Cutty Sark with Chinese food. The two of you really do think it's Chinese New Year."

"Ah, me. How hard it is to bring uplift to the provinces."

Elizabeth and I have cooked together for twenty-five years. It's interesting to watch what people do with that fact. More than half the time I'm the one who gets the *schwärmerei* about how marvelous the dinner is. But there's always somebody around who feels bound to come to her defense and who insists either that she's just as good a cook, or that she does most of the work behind the scenes. The first is true; but the second is undecidable. We really do work together. Except for a few specialities, neither of us does much elaborate cooking on his own. She will be busy right along with me all Sunday afternoon. Still, it beats being married to a golfer. I'm home for my hobby, if that's a blessing; and she gets to preside at the dinner table, which pleases her, I think.

(An explanation. About my alternation between calling her Liz and calling her Elizabeth. As far as I understand it, I use Liz when I'm just accepting her as part of the operation, and Elizabeth when I'm referring to her as estimable. I think I use the word "Madam" the same way when it comes to other women, but there's probably also a note of courting in that. Sex rears its lovely head.)

In any case, she made a checklist of ingredients, and, as always, offered to do the shopping. At five, we called the kids for supper, had the usual hassle between two daughters about which one was supposed to have poured the milk, and ate. That spring, we had two of the six kids living out of the house, but we were still eight sitting down, the slack having been taken up by a boyfriend or a girl friend. Halfway through serving, however, the oldest came in with his—I believe the then current phrase was, Old Lady—for a drink. Two more places. And one more hassle over who fetches the silverware.

Business as usual

Great.

AFTER SUPPER, SCOTCH, ice and conversation till seven, then a nap for me. "Royal Fireworks Music" turned up loud to drown out the continuing battle in the kitchen over who stacks the dishwasher. At seven twenty-five, I am yelled awake by the belligerents. Telephone. Mather Hospital. Peter Anderson had another heart attack. Back in Intensive Care.

Peter was seventy-four, and one of the old-timers in the parish. In fact, practically the only old-timer left. I am a traitor to the modern world. I have been in the same parish for twenty-five years, and I have lived in only two houses in my life: the one I was born in (literally) in Queens, and the rectory I'm in now. The Goddess of Mobility does not find me at her shrine. But she's found the rest of my parish there. Correction. Make that parishes. By sitting still for a quarter of a century, I have had five congregations in the same church. It's like having a wine cellar. I have only scraps of the 49s left, half a case or so of the 54s, no 60s at all, a case of 69s, and a new shipment of 73s in the process of delivery.

Peter was a great wine in a good year. Every Sunday, year in and year out. A carpenter. A constant help. Nothing ever too much trouble, and everything done in the sweetest way: patiently, uncomplainingly and, above all, without gossip.

Gossip is what Christians take up when they renounce the world, the flesh and the devil and find they still have a hankering for a piece of the action. Every parish I know of has at least a double order of *Kochlöffels* and *Dorfbesens*. They can't pass a pot without stirring it, and they can't pass rubbish without sweeping it all over town. But Peter was their nemesis. He just took it all in and let it die. Talk about an image of how the Silence of the Word takes evil out of circulation! They bent his ear, just as they bent everybody else's, but he never passed along a thing. He would just waste their time, muttering his meaningless "Ja, sure" in a slight Swedish accent, nodding his head as they rattled on, and then he would drop their priceless trash into the incinerator of his silence. He had a perfectly good memory. It's just that he had something else even better: a quiet, deep conviction that junk should not be allowed to spoil anybody's party.

I buried his first wife, Amanda, in 1954. She was not the easiest person in the world to get along with. Having been raised with Scandinavians, I spotted her right away as a tough Swede. But he was as gentle as she was tough and, after thirty-two years of marriage, he laid her to rest with a good conscience and honest grief. In 1964 he turned sixty-five, retired, packed up, and took himself a trip, on which he met a delightful widow whom he wooed and won in short order, and brought home looking like the original beamish boy. Besides being a handsome, sociable lady who was smart enough to know a good thing when she saw it, Isabel also had a tidy income of her own. So Peter entered his sunset years by lucking out: First a new house, then, as if he'd been born to it, a new lifestyle. He worked forty-three years as a journey-man carpenter, but he retired into the ways and means of a general contractor. And yet he was never anything but Peter. The parish was simply delighted. It was enough to convince you that God was actually in charge of something after all.

I went up to the hospital. I had taken him communion that morning, so I didn't take the Sacrament with me, just the Holy Oil. Isabel was in the hall and went with me into the ICU. He was out of it. Usual assortment of wires, tubes and blinking oscilloscopes. She said the responses while I administered Unction. (I had also anointed him when he had his first attack eleven days before, but that had been a relatively mild coronary. He had been improving in the meantime.)

Back out in the hall, I asked her when it had happened.

"Just before seven o'clock. I was in the room, but when they all started working on him, I felt I should leave. That was when I asked them to call you. It doesn't look good, does it?"

"You never know for sure; but you're right, it doesn't look good. Are you going to stay here now, or go home?"

"I wouldn't mind staying if I could be with him, but they have a rule in there about only five minutes an hour for visitors, so there really isn't much point. I think I'll go home. My daughter-in-law is with me for a few days."

"Good. I'll walk you to your car. Tell you what. I have to make a call tonight. I'll drop by here later on and look in on him. If ten-thirty isn't too late, I can give you a ring."

"That's very kind of you. I'll be up."

We stood talking in the parking lot. It was a beautiful May evening. Light breeze. Warm. One of those rare, unhumid Long Island days when you feel that, for once, there isn't a blanket of moisture between your eyes and the landscape. The leaves looked crisp and clear in the low-angled light. She made a comment on the sunset, was silent for a moment, and then went back to the subject of Peter.

"When people marry late in life, I think they are quite aware that it will come to something like this, much more so than young people are. But if it's a good marriage, and you have your health and the means to enjoy it, you begin to think like a young person again. Then, when the inevitable happens, it's really just as much of a shock as if you were thirty. Emotionally, I mean. You still understand, of course, that it has to be."

I said something about the difference. How the sadness of it was the same at any age, but that in the young, the presumption of a long future led them into outrage at the frustration of hope, and, therefore, into problems of understanding that age long since gave up on. She picked it up.

"Yes. Like that poor girl down in Coram, I imagine. The priest's wife who just lost her husband."

"Anne Jacobs."

"I didn't know her first name."

"She's doing pretty well but say a prayer for her."

"I shall."

"And I'll call you later on."

"Thank you."

She drove off, and I wandered back to my car. Some remembered lines from Auden's Good Friday poem, "Horae Canonicae":

>...It is not easy
>To believe in unknowable justice
>   Or pray in the name of a love
>Whose name one's forgotten: *libera*
>   *Me, libera C* (dear C)
>   And all poor s-o-b's who never
>   Do anything properly, spare
>   Us in the youngest day when all are

Shaken awake, facts are facts,
(And I shall know exactly what happened
   Today between noon and three)
That we, too, may come to the picnic
   With nothing to hide, join the dance
As it moves in perichoresis,
   Turns about the abiding tree.

XVIII

Wednesday, May 23rd

Peter's condition stabilized during the night, and by Wednesday afternoon, he was actually a little better. I spoke to him briefly, gave him a blessing, and said I'd bring him communion in the morning. I asked the nurse in charge to make a note that I'd be in at ten-thirty.

When I got there on Thursday, he was completely alert. Would I hear his confession? I turned the two-colored stole over to the purple side.

"Bless me Father, for I have sinned."

"The Lord be in thy heart and upon thy lips…"

He was guilty, since his last confession, which was before Easter, of being impatient and irritable at times. For these, and for all the other sins he could not now remember, he was truly sorry and asked pardon of God and of me, Father, penance, counsel and absolution.

I just gave him absolution. What are you supposed

to say to someone like him? He confesses minor flaws in his most notable virtues. It's like listening to Shakespeare criticize infelicities in John of Gaunt's speech. You're out of your league, Arthur.

After I had communicated him, we talked a little.

"I don't think I'm going to make it this time, Father."

"That's not your business, Peter. Everyone's pulling for you. Just go easy. You've made it before."

"Ja, sure. But this is too much trouble. I've had a good life, and Isabel doesn't need a sick old man around her neck. I'm ready to go, whenever it's time. Jesus can do me a favor and take me."

"He already has you. And Isabel, and me, and the whole world."

"Well, anytime he wants to finish up my corner of it, I'll be happy to help. I'm ready to go."

"I know you are, Peter. You're great. See you tomorrow."

"Ja, sure."

Out in the parking lot, a Volvo had pulled up next to my Camaro. In my mind's eye a quick cut to the TV commercial: "Ve built them the vay ve build them, because ve have to."

Swedish craftsmanship.

XIX

Friday, May 25th

I LOOKED IN on Peter again Friday, but he was asleep, so I didn't disturb him. I thought at the time I'd drop by later in the evening, but it didn't work out.

Still Peter was in and out of my mind all day. In spite of the obvious differences between him and Ted, there was an odd symmetry developing between their two lives. I jotted down some more notes:

1. Both, as far as I know, made it with only two women in their whole lives: Peter, with Amanda and Isabel, but with no problems because it was all reconciled in his mind; Ted, with Anne and Pat, and plenty of problems, maybe even enough to drive him to suicide. But: Christ has both situations eternally reconciled right now. What does Ted have to do to lay hold of the reconciliation?

2. Careful though. Don't get tripped up by the easy out, namely, that Peter's situation was moral and Ted's

was not. Ted's is still reconciled in Christ. What do Ted and Anne and Pat have to do that Peter and Amanda and Isabel didn't? Or do you formulate it the other way around: What do the first three have to do that the last three already *did*, or perhaps, *stopped doing?*

3. The old answer to that is that they have to repent. In that case, the second formulation is the right one. Peter didn't have adultery to repent of, but that doesn't mean he didn't have other things to reconcile. His impatience, for example. With Amanda, that probably meant a lot of repenting. Ted just has to do it in a different department.

4. But while the old answer remains perfectly correct, it doesn't shed much light on how Saying You're Sorry and Trying Not to Sin Again does anything about the trash you've already dumped in God's dining-room. Repentance has to be re-illuminated by some better images than talk and will-power. How about repentance as a willingness to forgive everybody, including yourself: Anne lays hold of the reconciliation when she forgives Pat; Ted when he forgives Ted, etc.

5. And how about forgiveness as metaphysically identical with forgetting? Anne, presumably, doesn't know about Pat yet. In a way, she is reconciled to her right now, both in time and in eternity. When she finds out, however, she'll be unreconciled in time, and have to work her way back to her present state. But then it will be a matter, not of involuntary ignorance, but of voluntary forgetting. Repentance, therefore, as a willingness to forget what Christ forgets when he sequesters evil in the eternal

death of his human mind; an acceptance, as out of circulation, of what he has taken out of circulation; an agreement to stop insisting on what the Word doesn't want to talk about. Repentance as shutting up and putting on the wedding garment.

6. Another symmetry: Peter is ready and willing to die. His death, when it comes, will be at least as voluntary as Ted's was, maybe even more so. What's the different then? Why is his performance admirable and Ted's dismaying? Watch it again, though: Stay off the morality of suicide. If you're going to talk about the state of their wills at all, talk about volition only as it relates to death. Because if it's Christ's death that saves us, then it's the relationship of their deaths to his that's the operative mystery.

7. But more. Be careful not to say that the *fact* of that relationship depends on their wills—don't set things up so that the good boys get to die in Christ but the bad boys don't. All the boys die in him, willy-nilly. His death is not a legal fiction they have the option of invoking; it's a cosmic fact they couldn't escape if they wanted to.

8. Corroboration of that. Even in the old imagery—with the resurrection out there at the end of time—*everybody was raised*, the just and the unjust alike. If the resurrection has always been preached, not as a reward, but as a cosmic fact, why not ditto for the death by which he leads us to it?

9. Why indeed not? The Lamb slain from the foundation of the world. Click.

10. But then. What's the meaning of the biblical insistence that death came into the world because of sin? It can't really mean that death *as a fact* is an accidental arrival in the world. Death is no accident; it's the master device by which the natural order is reconciled into the ecologically balanced party it is. Take away death, and you don't just break the food chain; you annihilate all the links.

11. But if sin didn't bring in death *as a fact*, what did it bring in? Maybe death as a perversion of a fact? How a perversion, though? Perverted from what? Well, if Christ's death is the master pattern of death for all men, perverted from that: "No man taketh my life from me.... I lay it down of myself." Perverted from *sacrificial* death, then, maybe? Close, but no cigar. From *offered* death? Better. From *priestly* death: Christ as the High Priest, willing the death that Adam the Priest failed to will. Click. Death as *offering* was the original design of death for man; but it was perverted, because of sin, back to the merely animal design of death as *robbery*. Man became simply the victim, when he was meant to be both victim and priest. Click again.

12. Better yet. Death in Adam was intended as the device by which something vaster than the balance of nature was to be achieved: a cosmic device, not just an earthly one. "Earth and stars and sky and ocean by that death from stain are freed." Adam's death as the means by which the universe was to become the Holy Mountain where the wolf lies down with the kid, and the sucking

child plays on the hole of the asp; all our deaths as Christ's death right from the start, but rejected, fought against, ignored; Adam's natural end as the most important fact in the world but not offered up and, therefore, seen only as a loose end till Jesus; Adam, meant to die as Christ, but ending up only a failed priest, a dead duck.

13. But even more: Adam, Ted, Peter, me, six million Jews—everybody, the whole failed Priesthood of Adam—as nevertheless dying in Christ all along. Christ's death on the cross, not as a new departure, but as the old home truth finally laid bare. We all die like flies, but that's been a contradiction right from the start. And a real contradiction, an ontological crossrip in our nature; doing one thing and thinking we're doing another; effecting the reconciliation and pretending we're not at the same time.

14. Finally: Our inevitable death as the engine of the reconciliation; and the reconciliation, therefore, as unavoidable, the wedding garment as inescapable; Predestination to Life in Christ as the last truth, because we have worn the Death of Christ from the first. The only thing we can do wrong is continue the pretense that we haven't got a thing to wear to the party: Hell as the little boy insisting that *he* has no clothes on, when the king has dressed him like a prince; the Second Death as total, stupid introspection.

Click. Click?

All Ted had to do was die?

XX

Saturday, May 26th

I TRIED THAT on a skeptical theology class Saturday morning, and was accused among other things, of Universalism (not true: I've still got hell in there), Quietism (not really, but I admit I didn't cover myself adequately), and kicking the pins out from under Morality (which may be true, but it may also be necessary: I have no fear that the subject will go away—only a strong conviction that knocking it on its ass now and then is good for its soul).

At lunch I got mixed reviews from the faculty. Art Hellweg and Jim Bates were with me all the way as far as I'd gone, but obviously, I had to go further. Guy Ferretti got on my back for not explaining anything, just playing with images—to which I replied that playing with images was precisely what dogmatic theology was all about, but that I hardly expected a historian to appreciate the point.

Ed Lawrence wasn't so sure that I hadn't broken morality's back.

At twelve-thirty, Liz called: Peter had had a massive coronary and died. I phoned Isabel.

Her son was there with her; they had an appointment at two with the undertaker. I mentioned that the funeral would probably have to be on Tuesday, since Monday was Memorial Day, but that I was free for ten A.M. or two P.M. either day, so she could make any arrangements that were convenient. I'd drop by later, on my way home from school.

Back to the faculty table. Another glass of wine and a wedge of cheese. Art Hellweg had taken up the cudgels for me.

"...but he's right, you mustn't let the ethical considerations in too soon. Morality is the enemy of mystery. Think of war, or blood sacrifice. Give a moral theologian five minutes with war, for example, and he'll come up with a whole system for deciding when it's justified and when it's not. Or else he'll say that in the Christian ethic it's always, and under all circumstances, wrong. And pretty soon everybody will be agreeing or disagreeing—and two thousand miles off the mark.

"Because the first thing you have to do is look at war, not as a moral species, but as a historic fact. And when you do that, you realize that it's one of the strangest facts in the world. The moral theologian decides about war on the basis of what he thinks the warriors are trying to achieve. But war never achieves anything. It just goes on and on all through history, one decade's allies turning into the next decade's enemies, *ad infinitum*. War has no simple, rational purpose. War is a celebration of death. War is a sick romance with death. A demonic black mass of death which a fallen race keeps saying over itself, because it remembers deep down that death matters somehow, but it can't remember the white mass by which it's to be offered so it can matter properly."

Jim Bates took it up.

"Exactly. And the reason why Jesus was against war is not that he was a pacifist. He was warlike enough in the Temple. It was because war is simply a distraction from the right offering of death. It's a celebration of robbery instead of offering. The cross is not an exercise in pacifism; it's what we've always said it was: the all-reconciling offering of what Bill calls the master device—of the death by which everything goes home into the Trinity."

Art again:

"And the same thing is true of blood sacrifice. The first question is not whether it's right or wrong. It's, 'What's it all about?' Take animal sacrifice. It was invented back in the days when everybody killed animals anyway, just to eat: If you wanted chicken for supper, you got blood on your hands. But they knew that somehow, death itself was more than just a means to an earthly end, so they took a special chicken every now and then and poured its blood on a sacred stone.

"Even take human sacrifice, if you like. In that light, it's simply the clearest perception of the mystery. If you ask only moral questions about it, you come up with the answer that it's wrong. But if you ask mystery questions, then, by damn, your understanding is liberated from the ethical box, and you finally have something to say to people who are smart enough to see that the crucifix on your altar is a picture of a human sacrifice."

And then Jim:

"Think of the martyrs. They weren't the first saints commemorated by the church for nothing, you know. If you try to justify them on a moral basis, you come up with all the tomfoolery of hagiography—all those inconceivable, insurmountable virgins who'd rather die than say Yes, or those incomprehensible saints who weren't smart enough to invent the doctrine of mental reservation and who got fed to the lions because they wouldn't throw a pinch of incense on an altar. The church didn't venerate them because of their moral fiber. The silly hagiographers may have done that, but the church in her wisdom just did it because she saw Christ's death in their deaths and said, 'Why, of course!'"

I made the point that, after all, the Eucharist is not only a celebration of the resurrection, but a showing forth of "Christ's death till he come"—one endlessly repeated lesson in Death as Offering.

Finally, Art again:

"I can even conceive of suicide as within the offering. After all, the martyr dies by his own will, if not by his own hand. There isn't that much difference between a martyr and a suicide. Take Ted Jacobs. And then take

Saint Barbara. I know nothing about his case, but just for the sake of argument, suppose he was half out of his head and thought he was doing those he loved a favor by getting himself out of the way. How different is he from good old Barbara who go herself killed because she had a freaky notion that Holy Matrimony with a rich, respectable gentleman of her father's choice was *ipso facto* adultery against Jesus?

"Suicide is so close to Death as Offering that it's scary. In the abstract, I suppose it can still be called a bad idea, because it's probably seen as a way *out* of life, while true, offered death is seen as a way into it; but even that doesn't hold up. It makes sense for Christians and others who believe in life after death, but it doesn't explain why even non-Christian-offered deaths can positively take your breath away, too. Like Aragorn's, in *The Lord of the Rings*, or like the old Indian's, at the end of *Okla Hanali*. They just lie down and do it. And it's so gorgeous, it damn near makes you cry."

AFTER THAT, THE conversation drifted to the inevitable springtime subject at the school: the politics of getting the faculty's budget through the Trustees. From there, it went to politics in general and then broke up into separate dialogues. Turner Adams, the Bishop's Chaplain and general gopher, cruised in and wanted to know who had made reservations for the Diocesan Clergy Conference at the Concord.

"Why do we have to go all the way up to the Jewish

Alps to a have a conference? What was wrong with the Dune Deck at Westhampton?"

"Adams and his committee of freeloaders are attached to those three-day, midwinter trips they go on, ostensibly to pick out a site. It just so happens, they're a bunch of herring *mavens*. If you want to get the Conference back out of Solomon County, you have to get them off that committee."

"That's all right, Eddie Boy. Just think of the ecumenical aspects of it. Jewish-Christian relations are the in subject this year."

"It's not the ecumenicity that bothers me. It's that I can't stand watching you eat fourteen kinds of fish for breakfast."

"So sit with Benson Carruthers and watch him eat his All-Bran. We'll take you to the Pussycat Lounge at night. In Westhampton they roll up the sidewalks at nine."

"In Westhampton, the action is not on the sidewalks."

"You're bluffing again, Eddie."

"But you can't prove it."

I'T'S NOT A universal taste, I know; but I like priests.

XXI

Sunday, May 27th

On Sunday, I worked it all over again: death as the engine of the reconciliation, all death as Christ's death—plus Art Hellweg's stuff on the real significance of war and blood sacrifice. Audrey still wasn't ready to order a case of it, but she threw me one bone:

"Sounds as if you've arrived, via the side door, at Kierkegaard's 'teleological suspension of the ethical.'"

"You've got it backward, Love. Kierkegaard and I both use the front door: scriptural imagery. In *Fear and Trembling*, he got there via Abraham's sacrifice of Isaac; I get there by the death of Christ. It's just that he argued too long with Hegel and ended up talking like him sometimes. My simple, humble boyhood in Queens delivered me from the danger of sesquipedalian words and transcontinental phrases."

"Not always. But anyway, I still like *Fear and Trembling* better."

"So do I. But wait till I've been dead for a century."

"I can hardly contain myself."

"You've managed nicely, so far. Still though, thanks for the reference. You encourage me."

"Terrible. First my car breaks down, then I encourage you. It's going to be one of those days. Bye."

She trotted off, and I mingled with the coffee-hour crowd until it evaporated. Then into the sacristy to unvest.

Anne had not been in church.

Thank you, St. Richard Cardinal Cushing.

Neither had Pat.

When will that crowd up there learn not to overdo things?

XXII

Tuesday, May 29th

Peter's funeral was on Tuesday at ten-thirty. Amanda had been buried up at Cedar Hill in the family's plot; since there was still plenty of room, his grave was dug right next to hers. By and by, I suppose, Isabel will join them.

> The grave's a fine and private place
> But none, I think, do there embrace.

Still, the image of the utterly reconciled *ménage à trois* is hard to resist. I know. In heaven "they neither marry nor are given in marriage." But watch how you interpret that. Be very slow to solve the problem by thinking of the inhabitants of the New Jerusalem as having got bravely past the recent sexual pleasantness. That's an impossible notion by anybody's imagery. Whatever the resurrection of the body is about, it's about bodies. Even when it was figured as taking place in the hereafter, it always meant getting back *all* your members. And if you figure it as I'm trying to—eternal life as this present life held reconciled now in Christ—then you not only have an everlasting member, but some everlasting action, too.

In the opening out of the web, of course—in the eternal performance of the piece we are now only sight-reading for the first time, in the endless exploration of the mystery we are now giving only the most cursory of casings—we will no doubt be surprised to find how much more there was to it than we ever suspected. But we've been down that road before. Maybe in Christ there's more to it than making love, more to it than falling deliriously into romance, more to it than lying comfortably in an old marriage bed on a hazy day off.

Admittedly, it's hard to figure how, since all we've got are the present images; but for my money, it just mustn't be figured as a suspension of anything. A removal of restrictions, perhaps—of the exclusivity of marriage or of the irrationality of romance; or an opening up of possibilities—an ascent, through fun in bed, to the processions of the Trinity of which fun in bed has so far been the merest sketch. Anything. Just don't turn the Creator into a Castrator. Add on, don't cut back.

Amanda, Peter, Isabel. Ted, Anne, Pat. Invoke the instauration! Pat and Peter? Ted and Isabel? Anne and Amanda? Anne and Pat? Why not? Even all six—and you're still only at the beginning of the opening out of the jury-rigged philosophy that couldn't stand up to the weather. The point is that all that kind of thing, by necessity, is purely of our devising. No matter how good it is, it's got no more strength than we have; and most of the time, it's got a lot less. Still, we go right on trying to use it for armor. We build ourselves little philosophical Sherman tanks and drive around in them, pleased as punch at our invulnerability. But then the engine breaks down, or the treads fall off or the gas runs out, and there we sit, "one vast important stretch the nearer Nowhere, that still, smashed terminus" at which we are always, in due course, deposited, seedy and by ourselves.

There is only one thing for that aloneness and that is Jesus alone. Not faith in God, because you don't know beans about God for sure. And not faith in what Jesus means, because all you've got to filter his meaning through is an old used teabag of a mind that unclarifies everything. Not even faith in what Jesus said, because, even if he actually said it all word for word, it still gets to you only through your myopic eyes and tin ears. All that kind of "faith," unless you're unlucky and it doesn't fall apart on you, is about as much support as a rotten floor. The only real support is Jesus. Jesus, Jesus, Jesus. Period. Period. Period.

Ah! You want to know what I mean by that. And, obviously, as a theologian, I shall open my big mouth and try to tell you, at probably nauseating length. But not here. Here you get only the one thing Peter needed to know: Jesus. The one unfiltered reality—unfiltered because you don't run it through your mind; you just say Yes to it. Not Yes, *because*...; just Yes, period. Or No, period. As you like. The vocabulary of faith has only two words, and both of them are addressed only to a man on a cross.

Where that all takes you, of course, is matter for endless discussion. And you land right back in the theological tank-building business the minute you start. It's inevitable, and quite harmless; but only as long as you remember that nothing you say is any better than you are, and you're not so hot. So just Jesus. *Yes*, Jesus. *Jesus*, yes.

(While my alter ego isn't looking, however, let me slip you one really good theological tidbit under the table. The smallest, strongest Sherman tank in the world: *If Jesus, everything. If not Jesus, nothing.*)

Arthur! Why is it that you always hit the nail once too often? Now you've put a hammer mark on a perfectly good piece of work.

S o PETER HAD a dry, gala funeral. I wished I'd had a bottle of champagne to break on the coffin. It was a launching, not a sinking. After seventy-four years on the ways, he slips finally into his real element and floats free to the fitting dock, and open water.

"...earth to earth, ashes to ashes, dust to dust; *in sure and certain hope of the Resurrection unto eternal life, through our Lord Jesus Christ;* at whose coming in glorious majesty to judge the world, the earth and the sea shall give up their dead; and the corruptible bodies of those who sleep in him shall be changed, and made like unto his own glorious body; according to the might working whereby he is able to subdue all things unto himself."

That's the old imagery, of course, but so what? You can't take anybody's theology too seriously, especially your own. Use it all, discard it all; pick it all up again and start over. It never saved anybody anyway, so you're not going to do that much harm or good with it.

Just Jesus. Jesus. Jesus.

XXIII

Tuesday, May 29th

After the funeral, I went home, had some wine with Liz and my secretary, answered a couple of letters and stretched out for twenty minutes on the couch. Up at one. Phone book. D. DORR, DOOL, DON, DONAHUE. Damn! DONAHUE—See also DONOGHUE, DONOHOE, DONOHUE. A battalion! Three columns of New York City troops advancing eastward, and I don't know either how it's spelled or her husband's first name. I half-remember her phone number, though, so I hunt for the 732 exchanges, hoping there isn't more than one in the W section of Strathmore East. Finally: Donahue George 8 Waverly Dr-Corm. Check to the rest. No more 732 W Corms. Luck.

I drove down, found the house and knocked on the door. No luck. Win a battle, lose the war. Maybe later.

As long as I was down that far, though, I decided to

"No. That was the other half of my armor. I refused to speculate, and I got very good at it. By the time that bitch laid the whole thing on me, I was so sensitive to my need not to know that I tore into her before she got the name out of her mouth."

The motherlode of anger. Gently. Give it another target.

"Last and most important stupid question: Why are you having a hard time swallowing it?"

She sat bolt upright.

"Why shouldn't I have a hard time? My husband is in bed with another woman. What am I supposed to do? Sit home nights preparing a hero's welcome for him when he drags himself in at eleven?"

"I told you it was a stupid question. But seriously. Don't ask me why you *shouldn't* have a hard time. Just try to explain to me why you are having one. Think of me as a retarded Martian. Don't assume I understand anything. Make me comprehend what you feel."

She sat back and looked puzzled.

"I don't know where to begin."

"You mean you don't know what to begin with. You're trying to find the heart of the matter so you can start elegantly from the top. Forget that. You can organize it all later. Right now begin with anything. It'll all hang together."

She drew a deep breath, and took a sip of tea.

"Well. I suppose one simple feeling is hurt pride—knowing that other people will think I wasn't good enough or woman enough to hold him."

"Do you believe the last part of that?"

"The funny thing is, I really don't. I don't think I was all that bad. He was the one with the excuses. Even right from the beginning of the marriage, at times. But there were a lot more of them in the last few years."

"Then if you don't believe the last part, don't worry about what people think who talk through their hats. Sexually, as least, it's no skin off your nose. It almost never is, you know. Men don't stray because they can't get it at home. More often than not, they stray because they can't *give* it at home. *It*, and more. And, since facing that fact is not exactly the world's greatest ego trip, they are ready, without even knowing it, for a short-order repair job on their vanity. Which, because of the newness, or the excitement, or whatever, the mistress supplies as one of her principal services. It's more complicated than that, of course, but that's usually part of it."

Arthur! That is a very large simplification, unless you're about to maintain that all romantic love is nothing but an ego trip.

True. But this is hardly the time to suggest to her that Ted may have been metaphysically and justifiably ga-ga about somebody. Let's leave it at the straying-husband level.

She took some more tea.

"Hmm! Tell me, though—about other people knowing. Is any of this known around the diocese?"

"Not as far as I know. But you should just assume that

it is—or that it will be. Gossip travels sooner or later. But mercifully, it also gets stale sooner or later. In any case, though, stand on your own feet. Show the world one triumphantly unskinned nose. What else do you feel?"

She hesitated.

"Responsibility for his death, I guess."

"How so?"

"The other day. I said something about thinking I was handling him with kid gloves when really I was just sparing myself. That's true. I have a sad suspicion that if I hadn't been so busy keeping myself together by holding myself in, I might have been more of a help to him. It might have been better if I could have faced him with it and hit him with a rolling pin, just once, right in the middle of Roger Grimsby. Maybe all he really needed was Andy Capp's wife."

"Maybe. But probably not. He was a lot more complicated than Andy Capp. Look. There are two ways of addressing the feeling of responsibility. Both are legitimate, but only the second one really works. The first is to recognize that what was wrong with Ted was beyond any simple solution, just as what's wrong with you or me is beyond it. Life is not a comic strip. We're fantastically complex combinations of strengths, weaknesses and sins, all rather lightly pasted together. He was no mere adulterer, any more than you were just a wronged wife. The stereotypes are lies. All through it, you dealt only with the whole mystery that was Ted. You enjoyed, or suffered from, his strengths; you coped with his weaknesses as best you could, given your own; and you forgave his sins. Or if you didn't then, you should now. And all of them, not just the sexual ones.

"Which brings you to the second thing you have to do about the feeling of guilt. Having said that the problem was so big that all of it couldn't possibly be your responsibility, you have to admit that since it was so close to you, some of it at least had to have been your fault. I don't know what part that was. Maybe you don't either. Maybe you'll never figure it out, though it would be useful if you could. But in any case, the one thing you absolutely have to do is forgive yourself. God already has, so don't spend even ten seconds disagreeing with him. Put on the wedding garment and join the party."

"That's not as easy as it sounds."

"Makes no difference at all. It's a matter of life or death. Don't mess with guilt."

She held the mug of tea with two hands and stared into it.

"It's all so complicated. The church tells you that forgiveness is the universal rule, then it spends all it's time setting you up so that you'll think of practically nothing but guilt. You know another feeling I have? It started out as anger at Ted for leaving me the way he did; but the more I thought about it, the more it became anger at the while guilt structure the church surrounds everybody with. I know it's contradictory, but I can't help feeling that all the pain—Ted's torment, my anguish, his death, my pride—that all of it was totally unnecessary. Just a sad waste of time that could have been spent on happier days. From there on, of course, it's mostly intellectualization and my other feelings don't go along with it; but, for instance: Why did we both have to live in little private hells? Why did it have to be that, if he did something to somebody else at nine, I got gypped out of equal treatment at eleven-thirty? When he felt good, he was very, very good. Why did the church have to make him feel bad?

"I once read something by a black woman about her straying husband. She said, 'He never gave nothin' away he didn't bring home again, honey,' so she wasn't complaining. Why weren't we allowed to be that relaxed? Ted might be pulling up in the driveway right now. I'll tell you something. If I could just hear him slam the car door, I almost think I wouldn't care if he'd had half the women in the parish. I'd get him a beer, and wait him out. It's not worth dying for."

"Oh, Love. You have just fired off a twenty-one-gun broadside. I hope I can remember it all, because it's good for a week's worth of non-stop thought in all directions. Let me give you just one reaction.

"I don't know about adultery. That's so fouled up with the demonic notion of people owning people that I draw a blank on it. But I can do something with infidelity. You have to start out by talking about fidelity, though. The doughnut instead of the hole. And you have to define fidelity as a faithful, attentive openness to another person. Infidelity, then, doesn't mean violating some framework around a person, called The Marriage Vow. It's a failure to attend to the mystery of the person inside the frame. On that basis, Ted could have been totally faithful to you, no matter who else he slept with. And vice versa. Totally unfaithful, even if he never looked crossways at another woman.

"You know? Marriage is the only place where we allow such a freaky definition of fidelity. For instance: You're under an obligation to be faithful to your children; but if anyone told you that meant exclusivity, you'd tell him he was preaching vice, not virtue. Just because you delight in one of them, doesn't mean you're under some solemn obligation to stop delighting in the other. The mystery of each one of them has to be pursued.

"Same thing with friends, parents, brothers, sisters. Faithful, attentive openness to every last one. Love is not a seven-ounce bottle of beer you can give to just one. It's a whole brewery which is supposed to be run at full production, with expansion as necessary. It's wisest, I suppose, not to try to act too fast on that as far as marriage is concerned, since all of us are hung up on the old exclusivity syndrome, and we're mostly lousy lovers and attenders besides. Maybe it can only finally be true in heaven. But even so, it seems to me that it still is the truth. What we've got now is just an incredibly whacked-up version of it."

She observed that her feelings went along with all that better when she said it than when I did—that I made it sound awfully free-wheeling. I conceded the point but said that liberty isn't necessarily either a virtue or a vice—just a condition of doing some very important, if expensive, business.

"Anyway. In the meantime, the forgiveness list gets one, possibly two, more names added to it. Ted, and yourself; and then the church, for screwing up screwing, and then maybe even God, for making it all so horribly expensive. It doesn't look as if it's worth dying for. But he goes right on insisting that it is. The only thing that takes the curse off it all is that he's willing to die for it himself. It's not a very consoling consolation, but it is The Consolation. Someday, let me show you some of the stuff I'm working on about death as the real instrument of the reconciliation."

She smiled.

"You do get back to your subject, don't you?"

"It's an occupational hazard. Or the nature of the beast. Anyway, it's fun—which I suppose is all you can ask of your trade. However, speaking of the trade, I really must run. Thanks for the tea."

"Thank you for the chance to talk. It's a relief to have it out. You have no idea."

"A little maybe. I actually had a problem once. Only one of course, so I can't claim vast experience; but I know the feeling."

"You're doing the funny-possum act again."

She hugged me.

XXIV

Tuesday, May 29th

I GOT INTO the car and looked at my watch: two-thirty. I had thought I might try Pat again, but at the moment I didn't feel much like it. I drove north to Whiskey Road, went east till I hit the unpaved section through the woods above Middle Island, pulled over to the side at a shady place, and turned off the ignition.

Lots of questions. Anne, Ted, Pat. If we are all such pains to each other, why do we bother? If love is such great stuff, why is it that most of what you hear from lovers is bitching? How they miss each other, how they can't stand each other; how life has conspired to keep them apart, how life has saddled them with the burden of being together. Ted aches for Pat; Pat is more than he can bear. Anne wants Ted; Ted doesn't know what he wants. What bunch of prizes! You wonder what made any of them worth the price of admission. Why didn't they—why don't we all—just cash in our tickets and leave? God knows. The power of the Mystery, perhaps, hidden in the romantic intimation of it? The gorgeousness of the City, hinted in the marital image of it? Whatever it is, it's obviously stronger than pain. Love as strong as death. "Stay me with flagons, comfort me with apples, for I am sick of love." Right on, Solomon. You and me both—besides your girl friend, and not counting Bob and Carol and Ted and Alice. Next time you lay something on God up there in heaven his dwelling-place, remind him that in the opening out of the web, he's got to make it pretty good to get rid of the curse of all this *tsouris*.

Remind him also to do something about his image. The church's PR job on him sounds as if it had been worked up by an agency full of dons. God as the Great Mafioso in the sky; God the Father as the Godfather. The church as *totus Christus, caput et corpus*, but Christ as the *capo di tutti capi*. Guilt as ineradicable. Judgement as the doom of self-destruction. Kiss the sinner and hand him the old family shotgun in the embroidered silk bag. BANG! Then silence forever. But not the reconciling Silence of the Word. The silence of *omertà*. The silence of the perpetually canceled party. Life as tragedy. I will remember their sins and their iniquities forever. The tyranny of goodness over a world that cannot be good. The impossibility of forgiveness.

Goodness, morality, as seduction from the gospel. Pay, pay. Set it right or die. But nobody has the price. There's nothing we can do. If it were only a matter of minor adjustment, we might make it with the help of the free-advice department:

> And, O my son, be, on the one hand, good,
> And do not, on the other hand, be bad,
> For that is very much the safest plan.

Look over the table setting before the guests arrive: The host's salad fork is crooked; straighten it. Wipe one spot from a claret glass. But it's not like that. The ceiling has fallen down, and the floor has collapsed into a flooded basement. The party is beyond any help except the king's universal distribution of the wedding garment.

Job sits in the dust in the middle of Whiskey Road with sore boils from the crown of his head to the soles of his feet. No oxen, no asses, no sheep, no camels. No sons, no daughters. Only the messengers of total collapse, and the miserable comfort of moral theologians who are sure that, if he could only put his finger on what he did wrong...

But Ted curses his day, longing for a death which will not come, digging for it more than hid treasures. I was not in safety, neither had I rest, neither was I quiet; yet trouble came. Oh, that one would hear me! My desire is, that the Almighty would answer me.

Adam, aching with love for the Beloved who is his affliction, ascends in the whirlwind of dust. Who is this that darkeneth counsel by words without knowledge? Where wast thou when I was the Lamb slain before the foundation of the earth—when, in the bloody Silence of my Word, I reconciled Pleiades, Orion, Mazzaroth, Arcturus, the wild goats and the unicorn, the ostrich and the horse, the hawk, the eagle, behemoth, leviathan?

And Adam, in the emptiness of the pain-spent, lies in God's arms, beached forever by the wave of the Spirit who moves upon the face of all waters. I have heard of thee by the hearing of the ear: but now mine eye seeth thee. Wherefore I abhor myself and repent in dust and ashes. *O God, I love you. I love you. I love you.*

And the web opens out, and the exploration begins forever. *Jesus.* Fourteen thousand sheep. *Jesus.* Six thousand camels. *Jesus.* A thousand yoke of oxen and a thousand she asses. *Jesus.* Seven sons and three daughters. *Jesus.* Jemina. *Jesus.* Kezia. *Jesus.* Keren-happuch. *Jesus.* And in all the land there were no women found so fair… *Jesus!*

> All which I took from thee I did but take
> Not for thy harms,
> But just that thou might'st seek it in my arms.
> All which thy child's mistake.
> Fancies as lost, I have stored for thee at home:
> Rise, clasp my hand, and come!

MY HEAD FELL forward and I convulsed awake in a cloud of dust. A truck marked THREE VILLAGE SANITATION disappeared around the bend.

XXV

Tuesday, May 29th

My watch read 3:15. I turned the car around and drove back to Pat's. I parked behind her Pontiac in the driveway and knocked on the door.

A seventeen-year-old girl answered.

"Is Mrs. Donahue in?"

"Who shall I say is calling?"

"Father Jansson, from Grace Church, Port Jefferson."

Pat called to her from the kitchen.

"Who is it, Laura?"

"Father Jansson, from Port Jefferson."

"Oh. Well. Ask him to come in."

She came into the living-room and introduced me to her daughter. Another good-looking woman. A little round in the face at this point, but with her mother's bone structure and general build. Both were wearing shorts: Laura, cut-off jeans; Pat a one-piece terrycloth beach thing. Laura told her mother she was going back to her room to work some more on a drawing.

"I didn't realize you had a daughter who was so grown-up. She's very much like you, you know."

"I didn't tell you. Laura is my child by my first marriage. I was eighteen, and it only lasted a few months. He left while I was in the hospital with her. We were divorced."

She seemed a little awkward. As if my presence were something she hadn't planned on having to cope with. I gave her an out.

"I was just down this way and thought I'd look in and see how you were doing. If you're busy, though, I can dash along. Nothing earth-shaking."

"No, that's all right. But come out in the back yard, I was just doing a little gardening and fixing up."

I followed her out, helped her move two folding aluminum chairs to the far corner of the yard, and sat down. In the process, the reason for the awkwardness dawned on me: Laura had got to have seen Ted around the house dozens of times. Having another priest show up crossed some of Pat's sexual-maternal wires. She was good though: no effort at explanation until she was ready to explain.

"I didn't see you in church Sunday. How's everything going?"

"Oh, fine. We had a nice weekend. We went to the beach all day Saturday and I just slept in till noon on Sunday. Too much sun all at once, I guess."

"We went on Monday, but I'm a devout shade-worshiper. My theory is that if God had meant us to lie in the sun, he wouldn't have invented trees and beach umbrellas."

Funny how things work out. If you had asked me at one which of the two, Pat or Anne, would be the easier to call on, I would have said Pat. In fact, however, it was the visit to Anne that went naturally. This was like trying to start a car a ten below. My battery was threatening to run down before the engine turned over.

Pat's eleven-year-old son burst out of the kitchen door, carrying a baseball mitt.

"Mom, what time is supper?"

"Gary. Excuse yourself when you're interrupting. Father Jansson, this is my son, Gary. Gary, this is Father Jansson. Father is from the Episcopal Church in Port Jefferson. I know him from some church school meetings I used to go to with Father Jacobs. He was just down this way and dropped in."

"Did you know Father Jacobs? He used to come here, sometimes. Boy, did he ever know baseball! The whole record book. He could tell you who played in every World's Series, including all the pitchers. I used to talk sports with him. It's too bad he died."

"Yes it is, Gary. I knew him pretty well. But I'm no sport's fan. The only record I hold is for lying in a hammock twelve hours a day for a whole week a cottage in Vermont."

She laughed.

"Be home at six, dear. And no later. Do you hear?"

He said okay and ran off across the yard.

Church school meetings! She thought fast on her feet. Laura had slowed her down for a minute, but now that she'd thought up the explanation, she was in control again. She leaned toward me with her forearms on her knees and lowered her voice:

"You understand about the church school part, don't you? It's just easier that way. The two boys didn't pay much attention to my relationship with Ted. They liked him, and that was that. Laura is different, of course. We've never talked about it openly, but she knows there was more to it. How much more, I'm not sure; but for the time being, I don't want her to find out any more than she needs to. Maybe I'll go to Grace Church with her next Sunday. Kind of return your call, and make it all seem natural."

She was a born engineer. On one level, it was duplicity; but it didn't come off that way. She was so good at it, that it just boiled down to not giving people more problems than they needed. Everybody, including me, was brought into the conspiracy with no more and no less information than he personally required. Satisfaction all around. The world may be falling apart, but in her corner of it, she's still in charge. Admirable. A little frightening, maybe; but admirable. Poor, lucky Ted. I smiled.

"Pat, you're a genius."

"Not really. But there's no sense stirring up trouble if you don't have to. That's something Ted never understood.

Not because he wouldn't. He just couldn't. I used to tell him he had no sense of privacy. He seemed to think that everybody knew what he was thinking. Like when he would be on the phone with me, and other people were around. Even if there wasn't an extension phone on the line—even if there was no danger of anybody overhearing—he still thought everyone else in the room knew who he was talking to and everyone word they were saying. And it was the same in public. If I was saying goodbye to him with a crowd around, I could always manage to get my back to all the rest and then pucker my lips at him or wink. He never did that, even when it just so happened that everybody was in back of him anyway. I used to kid him about thinking his head was made out of glass. He hardly ever even met my eyes in public. I got used to it, but I never understood it. I just decided I didn't have to. When we were alone he was fine."

It occurred to me that I would love to know how this prodigious sense of privacy of hers reacted to gossip about herself, but there was no way to find that out. I went off in a different direction:

"Life is funny. Being really in love, I mean. In one sense, it's nothing but the world's biggest pain in the neck. You find somebody you think is the greatest thing since sliced bread and you fall like a ton of bricks, only to discover that the most beautiful being in the world has a bunch of traits you can't stand. Your dish of tea turns out to be three quarters tea leaves. And the very fact of your being so much in love makes them twice as annoying; you and it's usually a disaster. But they really do love. If you're a born manager, and fall in love with one of them, you just have to learn to hold onto your hat and grit your teeth. Because you really do have no choice, and you know it."

"That sounds almost like the voice of experience."

"I've talked to a lot of people in twenty-five years."

"You must have."

Anne would never have let me off that easily. Maybe that was one of the differences. Pat's perceptions were sharp, but she didn't throw them at you. She kept her own counsel; but she also let you keep yours. Privacy. The priceless blessing of the only child. The thousands of hours alone, without brothers' and sisters' noses in your life. A whole childhood with nobody except a couple of mostly avoidable parents pulling your wires. A completely proprietary adolescence, in which only you were the one who ran your insides.

Of course, it wasn't always a blessing. There was the curse of loneliness; and the bitter fruit of the curse, self-centeredness. But the sweet fruit of privacy could at least be grown. I don't know anything about Ted's family. I only heard that one line from his sister Joan, but she could have been a hummer: "Let me pry into your life, Billy Boy, Billy Boy." Your Business Is My Business. All Work Done on Your Premises. Glass Heads Guaranteed.

It's fascinating. The implausibility of Ted and Pat gets more plausible every time around: She gave him the gift of distance up close, and it hit him like Demerara Rum.

"You know? The more I think of it, the more I get the feeling that Ted's relationship with you wasn't what did him in. Maybe it was more his relationship with himself—something that was always there."

"I'm glad you said that. When I first thought about myself and Ted's death, I thought about it the way most people would, and I held myself responsible. But when I think about it now—just for myself and him—I really do think I was more of a help to him than not. And as I said, so did he, when he wasn't fussing. Maybe I'm wrong but I think he even fussed a little less. He used to say that maybe some of my privacy was rubbing off on him."

There was a joke there, but the best rule is: If you have to wonder, don't. With Audrey, there would have been no question.

"Well, in any case, there's no point in blaming anybody, because God's not in the blaming business, he's in the forgiveness business. I think it's best to see it all as positively as you can. He's got it all reconciled somehow, and when we finally step out into the reconciliation for good, it will be the positive stuff that he'll invite us to explore forever. If you believe the gospel, he's an even better manager than you are. He gets it all straight."

"I hope so. Sometimes I have to twist things to make them work."

"We all do. I told Gary that my world's record was in Hammock-Lounging in Vermont. That wasn't quite true. It was actually in White Wine Consumption during one week on Fire Island."

"That's better. Speaking of which. Would you like a drink?"

"Sure. I have a completely adjustable yardarm. I can put the sun over it with a flick of the wrist. What are you offering?"

"I've got Fleishmans or Vodka—or Chivas Regal."

"Ah! The afternoon goes down in glory. A little Chivas, no ice, if you please."

She went in, got herself a Vodka and tonic and brought the drinks. We talked for another fifteen minutes. Laura came out, thinking I'd gone, I suppose, carrying a poster-size drawing. Pat asked her to go back in and get the rest. She gave her an "Oh, Mother," but went cheerfully enough. I always shrink slightly when people want me to look at their children's work, but Laura's was good: a whole set of posters for the senior prom done in Art Nouveau style. I gave her a compliment. She took it with ease and went back in. Pat and I rambled on till my Scotch ran dry. By then, it was time to head for the barn.

I DROVE BACK up 112. Poor, lucky Ted. All those winks and puckers. Anne may have been not all that bad. She may even have been good. But there's still a difference between tonic, and Vodka and tonic. It's one thing to do one thing well. But when all systems are go... Care to guess who gave her to Chivas Regal?

I turned on the car radio: Mantovani. Ten thousand

violins playing *More*. Good Lord! On some days, bathos sounds better than Brahms.

I walked up the rectory path singing, "This—is the greatest love—the world—has known…"

Liz gave me a kiss.

"I hope it was good Scotch."

"Twelve-year-old, no less."

"Well! What would the poor, tired workingman like to drink?"

XXVI

Tuesday, May 29th

During supper, I had a phone call from a man who wanted to know if he and his wife could make an appointment to see me about a marriage problem. I had half planned to use the evening to make some notes about the Universalism, Quietism and Moral Turpitude I had been nailed for at the seminary on Saturday, but I put it off till morning and told them to come at eight.

They came. We talked. Typical edge-of-divorce situation. Profound non-communication. No agreement, even on facts. Hardly even any common facts left. They wanted to know if the marriage could be saved. I told them No, it couldn't *be* saved. They might, as a long shot, try to *save* it themselves, but that was going to be very expensive. I spent half an hour trying to make it sound so costly that they would either do the dirty deed and get it over with, or else be inspired to do something major about their marriage for a change. Off the pot or on. Just stop the drift.

Apparently they hadn't expected to hear that particular line. They listened. I spent another hour drawing them out on the subject of how they actually dealt with one another. They were each waiting for the other to get straightened out—putting all their hopes in drawn-out psychological solutions that might take years, instead of working at the essentially political compromises which were all they really had time for before the axe fell. Each one's big subject was the other one's problems. Toward the end, I forbade them to start one more sentence with the other one's name, and I made them promise not to use the third-person-singular pronoun for fifteen minutes. It worked. That is, it didn't work; which is the point of the exercise. They kept slipping back into the accusatory "he" and "she," and finally got at least a glimmer of what a rotten habit they were in. They left smiling. Could they come back? Sure, if they liked lessons in political science.

Long Island has three principal crops: potatoes, cauliflower and divorces; and my parish sits astride prime land for all three. Its largest occupational group is single women. Something about the economics of the area, maybe, or what Art Hellweg at the seminary calls the intellectual poverty of Long Island. They're no better or worse than women elsewhere, I guess, but they do seem to jump ship quicker. Maybe a bad marriage at $16,500 a year is a little more obviously bad than a bad one at $60,000. Or maybe most of us are simply boring each other to death, but only notice it when we can't afford expensive distractions.

Or maybe it's just the suburban system. All day long (and for whopping long days—the commute to New York is two hours, *one way*) they live like single women, even when they're married. Their coupled life consists of a little coupling after mutual non-communication courtesy of TV, plus weekends which are either frenetic, child-ridden, football-plagued, or a hassle. The rest of the time, they're on their desperate, lonely own. You don't have to drive a heap like that very long before even a used car looks good. They may not be the world's best advertisement for the Romantic Intimation of the Mystery, but they've got to be one of its principal markets.

I came out of the office, fixed a drink for Liz and myself and got talked into a couple of hands of bridge with the two youngest girls. We went to bed at eleven.

XXVII

Wednesday, May 30th

HERE ARE THE notes I made the next morning.

UNIVERSALISM

1. How much truth is there in the idea that everybody is going to be saved; that, in the long run, even the devil will see the light and join the party?

2. Theological rule of thumb: Most questionable doctrines are the result of aiming a whole truth at the wrong target; it hits the bull's eye, but it produces only a half-truth in the process. Example. The Bodily Assumption of the Blessed Virgin Mary: Mary is in heaven right now, body and soul, because, on account of her preeminent sanctity, God has made an exception to his general rules. Aimed at Mary, that doctrine is a half-truth. She's in Christ's fullness now, all right; but the part about the exception is wrong. The rest of us are in it, too. Aim the

doctrine at all mankind, and it becomes a whole truth: *Christ's got us all together forever right now.* The Assumption of the BVM, even if it's nothing more than pious opinion, is simply a sacrament, a sign of what is true of all of us. The resurrection isn't coming; it's here, because Christ is here. The so-called Last Things are not the last things on a time line; they are the Ultimate Things in the constitution of the universe: *Death*, by which he reconciles everything now; *Judgment*, by which he vindicates goodness now; *Hell*, by which he sequesters evil now; and *Heaven*, by which, at this very eternal moment, the everlasting party is a success.

3. Okay then: Universalism. What should it be aimed at? At individuals? No, because if you do that, it turns into a half-truth: it forces you to say something the imagery of Scripture won't support, namely, that the individual human will has nothing whatsoever to do with the ultimate universal feast. God is going to force you into the wedding garment whether you like it or not. He doesn't really give a damn about what you think. Which, of course, won't wash.

4. So don't aim it at individuals. Aim it at the constitution of the universe. Then it becomes a whole truth: Nobody is outside the working of the Mystery of reconciliation. Everyone is predestined to the party. And, not only that, everyone is at the party right now. But everyone has a choice *how* he attends the party. Those who accept the wedding garment of reconciliation are there *openly*, face to face; those who reject it are there *sequestered*, hidden in

the silence of the Word of God's human death, carried in the black hole of the eternally dead human mind of Christ. Hell is at the party, because Christ's eternal death is at the party, really present under the sacramental manifestation of his five wounds. Individuals do have a choice, therefore: Lay hold of Christ's death in your own death, and come out into his eternal life; or refuse to come out, and sulk forever in the darkness of a totally unnecessary Second Death. The host will always *let* you out of the spear-wound in his side, but he's not about to *drag* you out. He does give a damn what you think. Click.

5. Bonus. Even the worst doctrine of all, Double Predestination, gets a kind word said for it. Watch: God ordains some to eternal life and some to eternal death; he predestined some to Heaven and reprobates some to Hell. Aim that at individuals, of course, and it's simply monstrous; it gives you nothing but a capricious, cruel God. But aim it either at God or at the ultimate constitution of the universe and it's simply true: Everything that happens at the final party, everyone's place in the grand, eschatological festivity, is ordained by his reconciling will. Nothing and nobody is outside the Mystery of the inscrutable decree by which—not out of merit, right or goodness of our own, but only by his Grace—all of us put up our feet on Holy Mountain and drink wine in the kingdom.

6. Even Luther's paradox of the saved man as being, all at once, saved and a sinner still, *simul justus et peccator*, rings loud and clear. Those in heaven are no less sinners

than those in hell. And those in hell are no less "justified" than those in heaven. The Eternal Host has consigned all sins to his oblivion. The difference between the saved and the damned is simply that the saved are willing to step out and explore what God remembers, while the damned insist on hanging around inside what he forgets. But willy-nilly, in his remembering or in his forgetting, they're all at the party. The saved and all their sins. The damned and all their sins. It's the relationship to the Divine Forgetting that's the heaven or hell of it all.

QUIETISM

1. If God's got it all together already, why bother about anything? If it's all going to work out no matter what you do, why fuss? Just sit back and twiddle your thumbs.

2. Is that even a half-truth? Does it hit the bull's-eye on any target, even a wrong one? And if it does, what's the right target to shoot it at? Blank wall.

3. Additional theological rule of thumb. Some doctrines, especially ones based more on intellectualization than on scriptural imagery, are fatally flawed from the start by sloppy intellectualizing from fake facts. Try that.

4. Fake fact number one. "Why bother about anything?" is a purely hypothetical question. We all bother all the time. More salt in the mashed potatoes, please; less volume on the hi-fi; scratch a little more to the left, honey; get your politics a little less to the right. We spend our lives giving a damn. Admittedly, sometimes about

the damnedest things, but we do it all the time. I bother to stay alive so I can cook crazy Chinese banquets; Ted bothered to get himself killed so he wouldn't have to stay alive.

5. Why do we do that? Why the insatiable thirst to get things to work out? Blank wall? Not quite.

6. Next rule. The Job principle: When in doubt, blame God. Things are the way they are because he made them that way. Even whacked-up, evil things are evil only in the style he makes possible by the gift of their being.

7. Next fake fact. It's not all going to work out *no matter what we do*. It's the very matters we do that are going to have to work out. We are in on the act with God. He's not doing it *for* us; he's doing it *with* us.

8. Therefore, first piece of sloppy intellectualizing: Quietism drives an unacceptable wedge between God and man. The separation it implies between the two is impossible, not only because God works with man, but chiefly because man himself is actually in the image of God. Man is not only *from* God; he's *like* him. And at the depths of his nature, not just on the fringes of his being: He's built so that he *functions* like God. Within limits, of course; but that doesn't matter. It's the proportionality that counts.

9. Why do I bother, then? Why do I *care*? Because I'm in the image of a God who cares. And specifically, in the image of the Second Person of the Trinity, the Word, whose caring, creating voice is the root cause of my being.

10. Example. I see a grown man about to clobber a

you claim I'm insulting. In any case, I don't see your version of the gentleman in question when I look at my pews. Not that there isn't a decent amount of intelligence sitting there: Audrey is a match for anybody. It's just that all of us, Audrey included, are caught up in the mental bankruptcy of Long Island.

Our condition probably prevails elsewhere, but I know of no place where it's so starkly clear. We are—all of us, Jews, Catholics and Protestants—the legatees of each other's impoverished mentalities. The Catholics are the heirs of WASP sterility and rudderlessness. The doctors and dentists may now have names that being with "O" or end with "a," but I defy you to distinguish them from their Protestant counterparts of twenty-five years ago by any criterion other than the different church they stay away from. Everybody's real religion here is real estate. And, while Rabbis get paid better than ministers, they are the devisees of all the worst features of the Protestant parish system—up to and including rampant laypopery. And as for Protestants, we, like the rest, have it all together. Only more so.

We are the heirs of a Jewish liberalism which, from Roosevelt to Nixon, produced the modern presidency; the assigns of the jejune New York Roman Catholic conservatism which, generation after generation, has ground out a diet of fear-producing moralism instead of the gospel. We are the catch-basket for everybody's worst. You want to know what the future of Protestantism is on Long Island? It's black, as in Black is Beautiful. The first three letters of WASP spell WAS.

And that goes for Catholicism and Judaism too. Long Island is the triumph of WASP society. We all ask the same dumb questions, and we all live the same dumb life of waiting for the next fad to come along. Everything flourishes here: Women's Lib, Transcendental Meditation, Going Back to College at Forty, Tennis, Marriage Encounter, In-the-Ground Pools, McGovern, Nixon, Beards, Karate, the Conservative Party and the A.C.L.U. It all just comes and goes. Our poverty is like the seven lean cows in Joseph's dream: It swallows up our riches without a trace. It is an irremediable poorness of spirit, an unfillable vacuousness of mind, an insatiable emptiness at the heart of our life, a famine of hearing the Word. We don't know how to ask what to do next, so all we do is just the next thing.

I was expounding that to my secretary when Liz came in with wine and glasses.

"Time to cheer up. It can't be all that bad."

"It's precisely the *all* that is that bad. Lots of the parts are great. The mark of a sick society is not the absence of good stuff; it's the presence of the tapeworm of intellectual poverty that gobbles it up so it never nourishes the body politic. On Long Island, the greening of America consists chiefly of mold."

"What got him started on that?"

"A letter from some man who didn't like the last book."

"These touchy authors."

XXVIII

Wednesday, May 30th

A LITTLE AFTER TWO, I went over to Audrey's to show her the notes. She was in the kitchen, just starting to make bread.

"Ah! The Archetypal Woman. She is like the merchants' ships; she bringeth her food from afar. She riseth also while it is yet night, and giveth meat to her household, and a portion to her maidens. Bought any fields yet today, Love? Delivered any girdles?"

"So. I remind you of a freighter, eh?"

"You remind me of a lot of things. But confronted with those faded jeans you've got on, the part about making herself coverings of tapestry, silk and purple just didn't occur to me."

"Well, come up with some flattery if you expect me to read that thing in your hand. My tongue is not exactly the law of kindness today. My children rose up this morning

"Like screwing sheep, I suppose."

"No, Love. You've got to fasten your attention on something more obviously natural than that to see how the objection works. Take polygamy, for openers. There's no question that, statistically, it qualifies as natural. Plenty of societies have practiced it—and precisely as a moral system, complete with obligations to be nice to all your wives, and to keep them fed and watered."

"And barefoot and pregnant."

"Touché. Score one for Gloria Steinem, *et al*. Nevertheless, even though the Old Testament is not their favorite book over at *Ms.* magazine, it does say that God himself looked kindly on polygamy for a while. Now, of course, the official view is that it's immoral. But that's where the rub comes in.

"Because, when you say that, you're asking people to see as unnatural, something which looks for all the world like a natural arrangement. All they can conclude is that it has been pronounced nasty for purely arbitrary and authoritarian reasons. There certainly doesn't seem to be any theoretical reason why the Word can't be affirmative about a loving, caring, responsible sexual relationship with more than one wife—or with more than one husband, if you're pushing women's lib and equal rights."

She poured some more wine and thought out loud: But what they'll probably say is that it doesn't work out that way—that human nature is actually up to only one sexual commitment—and so it really is unnatural after all."

"Not quite. Your argument is about to die the death of a thousand qualifications. Even the church doesn't say that. It allows you to remarry after your spouse dies. Which is two sexual commitments. So you have to back up and say 'only one at a time.' But that's no help. If all our times are held at once in Christ's eternity, the 'one at a time' is always 'two at once' anyway."

"But then they'll give you the bit about no marriage in heaven."

"Yes. But how are you supposed to read that? Does it mean that commitment to others—at least the marital version of it—just gets abolished? Or does it mean, maybe, that only the restrictions of marriage—exclusivity and all that—are abolished, while the commitments go on forever getting deeper?"

"That's all very nice: But it still sounds as if you're setting things up so you can get away with something."

"Precisely the root of the objection. They're afraid that any relaxation of the conventional limits of sexual behavior, however natural, will jeopardize a system in which they have a very large cultural and emotional stake. Notice, however, the sleepers that get into the argument when they try to defend the system: They hold that certain specific genital acts are always and under all circumstances, contrary to human nature. But that raises twofold trouble. First, genital acts are not a moral species in themselves. They become a moral species only when they are considered as human acts. But when you say that, you open the possibility of looking principally, not at the genitality, but at the love, or care, or concern which it sacramentalizes, and judging accordingly. Unfortunately, however, that option isn't open to too many of riper, if no less eager, years. We have too many hangups and turn ons geared to the old restrictions to look with confidence at the freer prospect. And, for all we know, maybe the young do too, but just haven't run afoul of them yet. You know? It could even be that people are right about fearing the apparent permissiveness. Not because it's theoretically unjustifiable, but because, just practically, no one is ever really going to be able to break with the system sufficiently to avoid the mischief that messing with it causes.

"The second part of the trouble, however, is that, to one degree or another, we have already half-broken with it. Take wet dreams. In the old days, you were supposed to pray you'd never have them, because they were unnatural and therefore sinful. The line in the Compline hymn before bed-time,

'Tread under foot our ghostly foe,
That no pollution we may know'

refers precisely to what used to be called nocturnal pollution. Nobody knows what that means when they sing it now. But if they did, they wouldn't believe it. Nocturnal emission in males is as natural as the night is long.

"Or take masturbation. That was really bad: You did it, and then waited in terror for the hair to grow on the palms of your hands. Who believes that now? Have you ever given a lecture against masturbation?"

"Of course not. They crawl before they walk. As long as they finally walk, who cares?"

"All right. But look what happens when you get that far. The whole genitally oriented system of sexual morality was held together by one thread: All genital activities, except one, were sinful. If you allow a single act in addition to the missionary position between man and wife, the whole shebang falls to pieces. Watch: Your son masturbates. That's okay. But, if he can do it to himself, why can't some nice obliging girl do it for him? Why can't they do each other? And why not other ways? *Soixante-neuf*, here we come. You can halt the collapse only by appealing to the emotional and physical dangers of messing with the system. But that's arguing in a circle: You have already broken with half the system emotionally; and most of the physical dangers that are left nowadays are there only because the system says teenagers mustn't have contraceptives and Wasserman tests."

She sat back and shook her head slowly in disbelief.

"You have a genius for thinking your way clearly into total confusion. I think I'll get myself a *mantra* and retire."

"Good idea. Get two and I'll join you. How about a nice little island in the Bahamas?"

"Terrible. Confusion *alfresco*."

"Confusion anywhere, Love. And worse confounded, indoors or out, by our Great White Goddess herself, Romance: We may *avail* ourselves of whatever sex our particular accommodation with the system makes possible—from laughing at salty stories on up; but we *believe* in Romance. Romance, for us, is the system beyond the system, the Queen that sails as she pleases through the system and lets her subjects founder in the wake. She enthrones herself over the system as the all-validating reason for everything: for pining chastity or for instant defloration; for leaping into matrimony or for lamming out of it. And I, for one, don't think any of us, young or old, are about to dethrone her."

"I don't know about that. There's an awful lot of random screwing going on that doesn't seem much like worshiping at the shrine. What I think is, that the young have pretty well broken with it, and, for all I know, are better off for it. We'll never know, of course, until they start writing novels, but I bet you a nickel…"

She put out her little finger. I hooked it with mine.

"You're on. Make your check payable to my estate if I die waiting."

"If I lose, you'll probably throw yours in my grave."

"Naturally. A nickel saved…"

I poured myself another glass, and through fleetingly of Ted and Pat: romance riding roughshod over the system, trampling everybody in its path. Lots of ouches, complaints and screams of pain, but precious little real resistance. The goddess often railed against but seldom disobeyed. I tried to probe the reason behind my bet.

"You know why I think we're not going to shake romance? Because, in spite of all the nonsense, it really is one of the great discoveries of all time. You're right about one thing, though. Its connection with sexual morality is tenuous. It isn't really about sex, it's about persons. It's not just getting the hots for somebody; it's suddenly, in one blinding instant, being convinced that the person in front of you is a mystery of greatness opening out into a large Mystery still. You see the whole universe in the beloved, and you see it clearer than ever before. Dante sees Beatrice, and, through Beatrice, he enters the ultimate vision."

"Yes, but at the end, St. Bernard takes over from Beatrice."

"Fair enough, but I'm only talking about what happens here. And anyway, even Bernard is just another human being who, in the mystery of his person, becomes one more access to the Mystery itself. Maybe Dante even designed it that way, to take romance off the merely sexual hook.

"My theory is, that if the kids lose the concept of romance in the name of sexual freedom, they will have done themselves a mischief. Romance is practically the only fast, sharp perception of the greatness of our being. God says we're great because he makes us great. And he loves us greatly for that greatness. But most of us, for most of our lives, just fart around, acting as if nobody amounted to a hill of beans. We take everything for granted. And when we do finally decide to ascribe greatness to somebody, it's usually some soldier or politician with feet of clay and a cement head. There are only a handful of experiences in life where you see the real mystery of greatness, and they're all different from romance.

One is long friendship with a good person: Year by year, it slowly dawns on you just what a prize you've been dealing with—and gradually, the music of the spheres gets a little more audible. Another is looking at your own small children. That's a lot like romance because it's an instant perception; but it's unlike it because, first, there's no true reciprocity between the two of you, and second, you've still got all those years to spend wading waist-deep through adolescent entrails."

She held up her wine glass.

"You know something? That I'll drink to. Not to flatter you, but if you're not a genius, you still have a knack: First you clarify your way into confusion; then you confuse yourself back into making at least a little sense. You're a lot better when you're intuitive. After all these years, I'm coming to the conclusion that you're not an intellectual at all, just a smart guy—sometimes a wise guy—with an intellectual mask on. The intellectualizing, unfortunately, has probably become second nature by now so you'll go down to your grave doing it; but at least, if you keep the intuitive side going strong, you'll just die with it, and not of it."

"As always, Madam, your flattery is so judicious and full of demurrers, that it would turn the head only of one committed to the acceptance of any smallest crumb. As such, however, I shall take it to mean that I have been given a stay of execution and hired back as your resident pestilent priest."

"You'll do till something better comes along. But

remember. I reserve the right to pray for deliverance."

"And I, to pray against it."

"All right. A draw. Now get out of my life for a while, so I can make like the lady in Proverbs 31. I'll walk you to the door."

XXIX

Thursday, May 31st

WHEN I GOT home, there was a note on my desk to call Dick Jorjorian at his office. I dialed the number and, after the usual welfare department game of putting you on hold for a small eternity, finally got through to him.

"Dick? This is Bill Jansson. What can I do for you?"

"Bill, thanks for calling back. I have to be up in Port tomorrow morning and I was wondering if I could pick your brains about something over lunch at the Elks."

"Sure. Just give me a time."

"How about noon, before the place gets jammed?"

"Fine. Do I need to bring anything?"

"No, just your head. It's about some vestry business. I want to bounce a couple of things off you. Tell you more tomorrow."

"Okay, Dick. See you then."

I made a note to remind myself of the date in the morning, wondered for a minute about why somebody on Ted's vestry would want to talk to me about St. Aidan's parish business, and then dropped the subject in favor of dinner and the evening.

On Thursday, I parked in the lot behind Port Jefferson's chief claim to gastronomic fame, the Original Elk Hotel and Restaurant, and walked into the bar at twelve on the dot. Dick was already there in one of the booths, nursing a stein of Löwenbräu. Usual preliminaries. Sweet Vermouth on the rocks for me. No lunch. Soft-shell crab for him. When my drink arrived, he hoisted his glass.

"Cheers. To St. Aidan's vestry. All the king's horses and all the king's men. Unfortunately, though, instead of picking up the pieces of Humpty Dumpty, we're making scrambled eggs."

"Having trouble electing a new rector?"

"We haven't had time to have much yet, but the way we're going about it, we're guaranteeing ourselves a giant family-size package. You know Henry Zeller?"

"I've met him at Convention. Had a run-in with him over an antiwar resolution once."

"Then you've got his number. A pompous ass, with a mean streak a yard wide, and a wife with a tongue to match. We're supposed to go in and sit down with the Bishop next week, and a couple of us are afraid that if he's there, it'll all hit the fan. I didn't really invite you to lunch to pick your brains. I just wanted to sound off some place safe, and you have a reputation for keeping your mouth shut."

"What's Henry got the wind up about?"

"Well, first of all, he's appointed himself Mr. Big. He was Warden of his parish in Queens, and when St. Aidan's became a parish, everybody fell for his 'years of experience' line and elected him Warden at our place. He's a real disaster. The rest of us have never been on a vestry before, so he's the only one that's ever been involved in electing a rector. As far as he's concerned, we should all just shut up and let him do the job."

"Well, at least if the rest of you hang together, you can still outvote him. It may not be pleasant, but you have the numbers."

"It's not that simple. You see, besides his other pomposities, Henry puts himself out as a big buddy of the Bishop's. I don't know if there's any truth in that, but he'll probably shoot his mouth off to prove it when we meet with the Bishop."

"Shoot his mouth off about what?"

"How much do you know about Ted's death?"

"A fair amount."

"Have you heard any gossip about why he did it?"

"No. Some guesswork, but no hard gossip. Mostly just expressions of consternation and incomprehension."

"Well, we've got hard gossip on our hands."

He slid his beer halfway across the table, checked the noise level in the next two booths and leaned toward me.

"What Henry has the wind up about is that Ted was involved with another woman."

Watch it again now, Arthur. A few more weeks of this and you can get a job on the tightrope with Ringling Bros. Say something neutral.

"Ah! True grist for his mill."

"You said it. If he gets even half a chance, what he'll do is put together all his prejudices right in front of the Bishop and start taking pot-shots at Ted's reputation—and, indirectly, at all of us who supported him. He's already doing it all over the parish, with his wife working the other side of the street. You know: 'What we need here is somebody who isn't a knee-jerk liberal, somebody who isn't so high church, somebody who will keep politics out of the pulpit'—all of which, I suppose isn't anything people wouldn't expect from Henry.

"But when he gets it all bolted together, he fills the tank with some high-octane innuendo and it takes off like a 747. He slips in some thinly veiled remarks about hoping the new rector will be a man who isn't caught up in the permissiveness that's ruining the country, and who stands foursquare for the family. The bastard never comes out and says anything definite about Ted in public, but plenty of people know what he's talking about because he makes sure he gets the hairy word out in private. I'm just afraid that he'll start that line with the Bishop and spread it around even further than it is already. I don't want all of Ted's good work undone and his good qualities forgotten just because of a couple of errors—and I don't want Anne hurt any more, either."

I sat back and thought for a minute. What did he mean, 'a *couple* of errors?' Strange. Still though, keep it general.

"Right. Gossip is almost impossible to stop, though. Chances are it'll get to her sooner or later. And with a big-mouth like Zeller on the job, it'll probably be sooner. I can only remember one time in twenty-five years I actually stopped a piece of gossip. I chased it all over the parish like a case of VD. It took me a whole afternoon and an evening, but I finally got to everyone it had infected and told them I'd put the curse of the church on them if they told one more soul. It worked. But then, there were only five people involved, so your case is different. If I were you, I wouldn't even try to stop it. I'd just do two things: one, contain it; the other, discredit it."

"Shoot, I'm listening."

"Well, to contain it, you go after old Henry. When's your appointment with the Bishop?"

"Next Thursday evening."

"Good. That means you've got a week. How many of the vestry can you count on to stand with you on the 'Let's not hurt Anne any more' bit?"

"Nine, maybe even ten out of twelve."

"Good, you're home free. Get on the phone and get all of them you can to press Henry to call a special meeting early next week to prepare yourselves for the conference with the Bishop. Don't say any more than that to Henry till you get locked into the room with him, but get all your guys to agree that he has to be sat on hard, once and for all, on the gossip about Ted. If it doesn't come up, bring it up and clobber him with it. Tell him that not one of you is going to stay in the Bishop's office for one second after he breathes one word of it—that you'll all just apologize to the Bishop and walk out in disgust at his speaking ill of the dead."

"You think that'll work?"

"Who knows? The hope is that it won't have to get that far. People like Henry spend their lives trying to provoke a response from other people. They're usually such lousy communicators that, unless they're being obnoxious, they can hardly believe they're in contact with anybody. And the sad thing is that we almost always deal with them the wrong way. We ignore them, or we fob them off, or we even go along with them, because we think they're just hopeless cases. Tell me something. Have you ever argued politics with Henry?"

"No. He's so prejudiced that it's impossible for me to listen to him without getting angry."

"Ah, but. Don't you see? All you do by that is reinforce his isolation—and his prejudices. Swearing at him and calling him a bigot to his face would be better than ignoring him. At least someone would be saying to him, 'Hi there, Henry, I recognize you, and I think what you're saying deserves my full fury.' Don't think of what I'm suggesting as ganging up on him. Think of it as group therapy for the good of his soul. He's just going to get worse, if somebody doesn't give him the dignity of honest, open anger."

"Never thought of it that way. Maybe it's worth a try. What's the other thing you had in mind to do?"

The waiter came with Dick's lunch and we ordered another round of drinks. I launched into my theory about defusing gossip.

"Discredit the story. You can't convince everybody of course: The veteran gossips never need facts anyways. But there's a fair-sized middle group who can be convinced that they really don't know what they're talking about, and that nobody else does either. What you say is, 'Who really knows? Did anyone see anything? Was he screwing somebody on the sidewalk? Were they doing it in the road?' Make them tell you, and themselves, just what facts they know. What facts do you know for example?"

"Just that he was at this one girl's house very often, and that her husband left her, and that after he left, Ted was there at night sometimes."

"All night?"

"No, just in the evening."

"Did they make love in front of the windows?"

"No."

"Did her husband ever catch them in the act in a motel?"

"No. But Zeller says people have seen them having a drink together in the Elks here."

"Since when is social drinking in public a sin or a

crime? Haven't you ever taken your secretary or some female colleague out for a drop of the milk of human kindness?"

"Sure."

"Well, do you see what I mean? It's all circumstantial evidence and, more important, the circumstances could be evidence of something totally different, worse or better. People have such limited imaginations. Maybe they were Scrabble buffs. Maybe they had a prayer group going. Maybe they were into Zen. Maybe she was frigid and he was functionally impotent with anyone but his wife and all they did was *talk* each other into orgasms. Maybe they performed chicken sacrifices. Who really knows? Somebody got negatives?"

"Well, when you put it that way, the answer is, 'Of course not.' But you know what people conclude."

"I don't give a damn what people conclude. People have been lynched for what other people concluded. You're supposed to be running a Christian community down there, not a gossip pool. In spite of rumors to the contrary, the God we worship is not keeping score. Just try to get the reasonable types on your side by getting them to suspend judgment. It'll all blow over by and by anyway. And furthermore, it's just one whopping distraction from the job you're supposed to be up to, which is electing yourself a rector who will be half as good a priest as Ted was. Tell them, *ad nauseam:* 'Get on with the job; don't futz around with the past.'"

He poked a fried crab-leg into the tartare sauce and

tucked it into his mouth.

"William, you are a shifty character. A Philadelphia lawyer in priest's clothing. But I suppose you're right. Anyway, it's worth a try. Particularly the bit about cowing old Henry before we get to the Bishop. I'll let you know what happens. By the way, have you seen Anne since I saw you at the rectory?"

"Yes, as a matter of fact. A couple of times."

"How does she seem to you?"

"Pretty strong, considering."

"Does she know about any of this gossip?"

"Can't say. But knowing a little about the world, the flesh, the devil, and the general tone of your average Episcopal parish, it would be surprising if she didn't, sooner or later."

"I should correct myself. You are a circumspect, shifty character. Maybe that's why people talk to you. Just the right hint of thievish honor."

"Any virtue in a storm. But anyway, the whole thing really is a distraction: parochially, morally, theologically and personally. Nobody *knows;* so they should all just shut the hell up. If worse comes to worst, though, maybe you could throw yourself into the breach as a sacrifice and distract them all by having lunch once too often with that nice parish secretary down there right in the front office. Take their minds off merely circumstantial evidence."

"Your suggestions are sometimes tempting, even if they're not always brilliant. I think I'll stick to trying to cut Henry Zeller's balls off."

"Ah! Castration as the better part of valor. Listen, are we splitting the tab here?"

"No, it's on me."

"Well, in that case, mind if I have an *Ouzo?* Good way to start the afternoon. Besides, you owe me for this priceless advice. You did pick my mind after all. I feel positively deflowered."

"I imagine it's a little late for that. Waiter!"

XXX

Thursday, May 31st

THE REST OF the afternoon and evening were business as usual—some of it even old business: reruns on TV from eight to ten. After two hours of complaining about having to watch Doctor Wonderful and Detective Hardnose do for the second time what was totally predictable even the first, I told Liz I was ready for a short dose of crime and calamity on the ten o'clock news and an early bed. She shook her head.

"If you don't like escape shows, why do you watch them?"

"Beats me. Probably I'm a philistine at heart. Culture threatens me. Anyway, I refuse to watch Channel 13 until Port Jefferson gets cable TV. Invisible people mumbling in a pale blue snowstorm is not my idea of either uplift or entertainment. What's holding up the franchise?"

"The village fathers, I think."

"Why? Everybody around us has it."

"Who knows why? Maybe they're afraid that if they're not blocking at least one minor improvement at all times, they'll get out of practice and actually let a major one slip by some day."

"Ah yes! A man's inconvenience should exceed his comfort, else what's a village board for? I know what. I'll switch to watching television in the afternoon and make parish calls in the evening. The soaps are better anyway. Live actors and true-to-life dumb situations. Come to think of it, making parish calls is watching the soaps. I really don't need television at all. You know? When you make calls between three and four, half the time they don't even turn the television off while they retail their problems. You get two episodes of *How to Survive a Marriage* for the price of one."

"If you're going to talk, turn off the set; if you're going to watch, turn off the talk. If you're not going to do either, let's go to bed."

We watched about fifteen minutes' worth of Watergate, interrupted by the same Mop & Glo commercial two times running. The details about a dismembered body found near a Chinese laundry on the west side were just about to come on when the office phone rang. Usual dash.

"Grace Church rectory, Father Jansson."

"Bill? This is Dick Jorjorian. Twice in one day."

"Richard! What can I do for you?"

"Remember our conversation at lunch about whether Anne Jacobs knew anything?"

"Sure."

"Well, your stuff about defusing gossip wasn't delivered soon enough to do any good."

"What happened?"

"I'm afraid a cat outside the bag sprang the one inside right in front of Anne."

"How so?"

"Irene came in about an hour ago from a visit to the rectory. Some of the Episcopal Church Women had the bright idea of paying Anne a social call—visiting the fatherless and widows in their affliction and all that. Unfortunately, Zeller's wife went along. Nosey Parker."

"What'd she say? She didn't just come out with name and address did she?"

"No. But she might just as well have. She started this general conversation about people in the parish, and who was and wasn't coming any more. And then she asked if anyone knew whatever happened to the good-looking young woman who kept the church school records. (I didn't fill you in on that, but that was the one Ted was seeing.) Anyway, Irene tried to change the subject, but there was one innocent there who fed Madelene Zeller straight lines, and it was a good couple of minutes before the matter got dropped. Irene said she watched Anne like a hawk as soon as it came up. According to her, Anne damn near fell apart on the spot. She checked with one of the other gals afterward, and she thought the same thing. We've been talking about it ever since Irene came in, and, obviously, I mentioned seeing you at lunch. She's of the opinion—and I agree with her—that if there's any way you could manage to drop by and see Anne, it might be a good idea. Any chance of that?"

"Sure, I guess. You don't mean tonight, though, do you? That's a little bare-faced."

"I hadn't thought when. Only soon."

"Give me a second to think."

I fished for an excuse for going down there on Friday when I'd just been there on Tuesday.

"Well, maybe something about that low-income housing business. Like wanting Ted's file on it because a friend of mine somewhere was interested in what we'd done, and I'd thrown my stuff out the last time we went through the files here. Sound too fishy?"

"No. Just do it soon. Irene is no alarmist. When she gets alarmed, that's enough for me."

"I'll try to set it up for tomorrow morning."

"Good enough. Let me know if I can help. And thanks."

I hung up and debated the merits of calling her right away. I was leery of it, but in the end I decided that giving her to whole night to think of the possibility of talking was better than some short-order arrangement in the morning.

So I called her, rattled off a spiel about this priest friend of mine who was up against the same situation we'd found ourselves in, and wondered if I couldn't drop by tomorrow morning and borrow the stuff in Ted's file. I apologized for calling so late, fabricated some more details about the urgency of it all, crossed my mental fingers, and shut up.

She said it would be all right.

I let out another gusher about whether ten would be too early and how I hoped it wasn't inconvenient.

She said No, it was all right.

I thanked her, wished her goodnight, pushed down the phone button with my finger and crossed myself with the handset.

God!

Give her something, because whatever it is, it isn't going to be a good night.

Head still down, she said, "What do you mean?"

"Want to try to talk your way through it?"

"What good is talk?"

"Who knows? Since it's all we've got at times like this, why not give it a chance?"

She sat up.

"Well, it's your trade. You talk first."

"Okay. Look. Whatever else this is, it seems to me that at least it's got the virtue of being the last piece of bad news. Whatever it was you were keeping yourself from is finally out on the table. Try to grapple with it."

"What do you mean, grapple with it? I've just spent that whole night doing exactly that."

"Do it again. This time you've got an audience."

"What's the use?"

"Try, Love. Try."

She put her head down again. Long silence before she finally sat up. She breathed out hard.

"Okay. I was in love with Ted. I bore him two sons. I thought that I mattered, that I had a place in his life. What does it say about me that he took up with that… well, broad?"

"That's a loaded question. Listen. Words of one syllable. She can't possibly be only a broad. That's not really conceivable, is it, knowing what you know about Ted?"

"It's as far as I've been able to get."

"Well, try to take it further. Ted was a complicated piece of business. Not only to himself, but to everyone else who ran into him. We all are, I suppose. But he was a kind of deluxe complication. He had a tragic view of life. In spite of all his enthusiasm for knitting up the wounds of the world, he was always more aware of the unraveling than the knitting. Do you know where I found the low-income housing file? Under *Lost Causes.*"

"Figures. He always took everything hard. But why her? What does it say about me?"

"Words of one syllable again. That's not the world's greatest question for you to be asking. If you want an answer, I would say, very little. But if you want my opinion about what you really need, you need to talk to yourself like a Dutch uncle and remind yourself that you're not the main subject here. Neither is his mistress and neither am I. We've talked around the main subject for a month. It's Ted. Somehow peace has to be made with him and in him before the rest of us can get any rest."

"What do you mean? He's dead."

"No he's not. First of all he's alive in you and in her—and to a lesser extent in others. But more important, he's alive in Christ, if you believe the stuff we say we believe. And if that's true, then all the unreconciled business in this whole mixed bag—you and Ted, you and she, she and Ted and, above all, Ted and himself—all that has got to be put together somehow by all concerned, because Christ has got it put together already and anybody who resists the reconciliation is going against the grain of the universe."

"So I'm supposed to be reconciled to her? In order to somehow patch up Ted? How does that work?"

"I don't know. I only believe it. He couldn't get himself together while he was alive; but everything about him is going to be put together willy-nilly. Since the two of you were very much about him, the heat is on you to put on the wedding garment of reconciliation, or else get left out of the party—maybe even, God knows, keep him out of the party. We're not really separable from one another."

"Well, he seemed to keep us pretty well separated."

"That's highly debatable. I would say he kept you pretty badly separated. So much so that he tore himself to pieces in the process. Look. You're the only one who saw the suicide note. What did it say?"

"I know it by heart: 'Darling, I'm sorry I'm not better than I am, but I can't go on this way. Forgive me. This is the only thing I can do. All my love.' That was it. No names. It wasn't even clear whom he had in mind. What am I supposed to do with that?"

"Obviously, you're supposed to do something with it that he couldn't. Like maybe being able to get all the names—all the persons—back into the act as much as you can. His problem was that he had two names he somehow couldn't say together. But the two of you are at least in a position to deal with it differently. Each of you held *him*. Maybe only a part of him as far as he was concerned, but if I know anything at all about women's loves, you each meant to hold all of him as far as you were concerned. The two of you overlap—and you overlap precisely where he was divided. Your reconciliation with each other has just got to be one of the instruments of his reconciliation with himself."

"What am I supposed to do, run over to her place and throw my arms around her?"

"No. But you've got at least to hold open the possibility of something like that if the circumstances are ever right. Maybe it's hard to contemplate emotionally, but there's a certain logic to it. After all, you both had your arms around him. Think of all the arms as squeezing him back into one piece. It's a better image than the picture of two women holding half a man each with one arm and pushing themselves apart with the other. Make love, not war. The war inside Ted has got to end somewhere."

She put her head down on her arms once more and said nothing. After a while she began to cry quietly. I sat still for a minute, then got up, went around to her side of the table, drew her to her feet and put my arms around her.

"What are you crying for, Love?"

She buried her face against my shoulder.

"You know? I've cried a lot since the funeral. But I think this is the first time I've cried for Ted and not myself—for the sadness in him and not just for the sadness in me."

"That's a big step. Don't underestimate it. It's the unlocking of a prison. Maybe even for him."

"Do you really believe that?"

"All I know, Love, is that I want to believe it. Which

is about the best you can do on most days. You all right?"

"Yes."

"Well then, let me dry your tears."

She looked up at me. I kissed both her eyes and wiped her face with my beard.

"Ted used to do that."

"It's one of the advantages of men with beards."

"Yes."

She kissed me.

"Thanks for coming."

"Any time."

"Hey! Don't forget the folder."

"Feeble-minded Freddy, that's me."

"Don't worry about it. You have other virtues. See you soon."

"Good."

XXXII

Friday, June 1st

By the time I got back up to Port, I had a headful of questions. I drove to the harbor, parked at the edge of the marina and shut off the engine. High tide. Elephant-gray sky and water. Couple of tugs warping an empty tanker into position to head out.

When I left Anne's, I thought for a minute about going over to see Pat, but I had a confused reaction to the idea. Too much like Tuesday. Charleyhorsing the long arm of coincidence twice in one week. Don't go poking around just out of curiosity. If she needs to talk, she'll call.

On the other hand, how do you know? Except for the first time I met her, all the subsequent sessions were at my instigation. Maybe she feels the rules of the game are that the initiative is supposed to be in my hands.

Once again, though, what game? Actually, she seems to have squared herself away pretty well on her own.

What am I doing? Why the big rush to jump into Ted's shoes and get involved with both of his involvements? Because that, Arthur, is exactly what you're doing. Think up as many fancy theological justifications for it as you like, the fact remains that his two clock-winders are beginning to get to you. And what's your clock wired to? Dynamite maybe?

God, what a pain! Sometimes I get tired of lecturing poor, dumb Arthur. What's so antithetical about sexual attraction and fancy theological explanations? Why do I have to *accuse* myself of leching my way into Ted's shoes? Suppose God wanted me there for some reason—to offer up his pain, say, or to bear the anger he couldn't—who's to say he wouldn't use sex to draw me in? As a matter of fact, if it's a question of drawing *me* in, that's probably the exact method he'd pick. Save himself work. He'd be a long time luring me into position if all he had for bait were Ted's interest in baseball and civil liberties.

You do have to admit, though, Arthur, that the several effects of these two women are not what you'd have expected. Here you are, for the second time in a week, sitting alone in a car after a visit to Anne, having decided, for whatever reasons, not to visit Pat. She's obviously the *dish*. Why is it that Anne turns you off her? Why are you here watching tugboats instead of down at her place? Why does the situation with Anne strike you as more *romantic?* The luscious chemistry of grief, maybe? Or some deep-seated predilection, out of God knows where in your background, for sad apples? If it's that, though, the question comes back again, why Anne? Pat was a sad enough apple when you first met her. Why the pit-of-the-stomach reaction to the guy's widow and not to his mistress? Why the out-of-character response? Why aren't you more wound by the looker with the Chivas Regal who sends you on your way singing *More?* Why is the one who has obviously been handled so untouchable and the chaste one so accessible?

You want to know why, Arthur? It's because there's no liberation from romance. From sexual restrictions, maybe, but from the romantic bind, never. It's just not in the cards your upbringing dealt you.

Marriage, the big, fat, permanent institution, ends. Pfftt! Just like that. New ballgame. But romance, the shaky, fragile, practically insupportable contraption goes on forever. In your mind, Pat *belongs* to Ted in a way Anne doesn't. She's *taken*. Morality to one side, you can conceive of having something going with Anne. Something with Pat is unthinkable.

But that's dumb any way you come at it. If you stay clear of both of them in the name of morality, you end up dealing at a distance with people you're probably called to be close to. And if you move in closer, you end up playing Ted with the shoes on the opposite feet: This time maybe the mistress gets the short end of the stick.

Marvelous vision: Myself as Ted going through it all again in reverse. Vicarious lust to put me in a position to make the vicarious repentance that springs him out of whatever prison he's locked in. Vicarious angers, hassles and pouts to somehow bear into the Passion what he could only fling down in fury. And you know? While that's probably not the way the front office would advise you to proceed if you asked for permission, it is still absolutely one of the ways of doing it. It's barbaric and immoral, and a damned peculiar way to run a universe, but if even one pair of shoes is outside the power of the reconciliation, then the universe isn't being run at all—which is a possibility, but I choose not to think of it. The point is, if it's run by the vicariousness and substituted love we believe in, then *every* substitution becomes efficacious in Christ. Who's to say you can't bear others' burdens *without limit:* not only their pains in your pains, but their sins in your sins?

Ted's lust, Ted's anger. If they're going to be offered up for reconciliation, they're going to have to be offered by someone capable of them. Someone who can take their measure. Me for the lust maybe, and Anne and Pat for the anger? Or maybe I get it all, and just haven't come close enough yet to feel the anger.

In any case, who's to say that it's only sweetness, light and pure thoughts that are intercessory? Are only the good deeds of the saints salutary? Is their glorying in their infirmities just a big Uriah Heep act? Or are they the only ones who understand that all our righteousnesses really are filthy rags, that sin is everywhere, and that the only available intercessors here are sinners every one. Nobody, I suppose, is literally invited to screw his way into the New Jerusalem; but given amazing, dumbfounding grace, it's probably been done fairly often. At a price, no doubt. Lord Rochester died of old age at thirty-three. Vice as sacrament. Incredible!

Fear and trembling. The utter universality of the Mystery, the Underweaving, the Drawing. The Hugeness that holds us no matter what we do. The awful weight of what, on one bright afternoon, we lift with such light minds. The certainty of the Supper of the Lamb and the total impossibility of any free lunches beforehand. The world, not as some two-bit system of cranks and levers to be dabbled with at arm's length, but as an absurd envelope of relentless love in which we are caught, sealed and sent home forever. Driven up and down in Adria by the blasts of a foolish Wisdom, anchors up, rudderbands loosed, mainsail to the wind, hinder part broken with the violence of the waves. No help for it but swim who can.

And some on boards and some on broken pieces of the ship.

Ted and me, safe to land, on opposite ends of the same jib boom.

THE TUGS BACK away from the tanker and head in. Loud blast from her foghorn and a plume of dense black smoke from her stack. Screws churning the water as she starts toward the mouth of the harbor. Time to head in myself, look at the mail, and have a glass of wine with Liz.

Jesus. Jesus. Jesus.

XXXIII

Friday, June 1st

At twelve-thirty, I asked my secretary to give me half an hour while I stretched out on the office couch for a nap. At one, I got up, went straight to the phone, dialed Pat's number and asked her if she was going to be in for the next hour or so. A foolish consistency...

By the time I got there, I had thought my way through a string of conversational openings, only to discard them one after another. When I rang the doorbell I had no more ideas in my head than I had in my forefinger. She let me in.

"Hi. It's nice to see you."

"Nice to see you, Pat. Not that I know exactly why I'm here. Just felt like talking I guess."

"What about?"

"Ted, I suppose. Or my own thoughts about it all. You

might say that between one thing and another, I've had a Ted week. Funny how some things take time to catch up with you. They're in your mind but you don't start sorting them out until you've held onto them for a while. I suppose I just wanted to compare the state of my sortings with the state of yours."

"Well, come sit down. I can't offer you a seat outside in this weather, but can I get you something?"

"No, not now, thanks. Maybe later."

I dropped into an armchair and she took the sofa. White bodyshirt, pale blue slacks, sandals kicked off. She sat erect in the corner, legs tucked under her, the lines of her body rounded and taut. Womanish and girlish at once. Nice.

"What were you thinking about Ted?"

"Remember I said I thought that somehow it was his relationship with himself that did him in—that his relationships with others were simply contributory to something that was always there? Well, I was thinking this morning that maybe there was a kind of deep anger in him—possibly out of somewhere in his past—and that in his case it's the reconciliation of that anger that's the key to our all getting wherever it is we're supposed to get.

"Look. This is straight off the top of my head. But for instance. Take his gentleness. That was the quality most people noticed, and there's no question but that it was real. But maybe, for all its reality, it never did sit comfortably on him. Maybe it was like a lid on a pressure cooker: strong, but dangerous. Because the way he died was the exact opposite of his gentleness. It was violent to himself, and it was violent to everybody else concerned. Maybe you could even say that his death was a kind of reverse offering—a flinging down rather than an offering up of the violence he couldn't handle—that it was, in its own way, an attempt to do something, well, *holy* with it. If that's not stretching the word 'holy' too far."

"I don't think it is. I never said much about his anger to you but I felt it a lot. It rubbed off him onto others, I think. If you ever pressed him, you found yourself getting angry at his responses. You know what surprised me after the first time I talked with you?"

"No, what?"

"That I spent so much time in the midst of my grief telling you how angry I was with him. Not just over his suicide, but over the little details of the anger which was inside me during my love for him. I hadn't planned to go on like that. It was just sort of there, waiting for a chance to get out."

"The pressure cooker again."

"Yes. But getting it out doesn't solve all the problems. Because you know what comes after that? Sadness. Sadness at the two of you having shared a love that was the greatest thing either of you ever knew, and yet somehow, not being strong enough, or good enough, to make it work. I was never sorry for having loved him all those years, and I'm still not. But I am sorrier than I ever was about anything that somehow the best thing in my life—the thing I cared most about in the whole world—was the very thing that, because of me and him, because of the kind of people we were, I finally couldn't do at all.

"And when you realize that, the anger comes back again. Anger at a world which makes you fail at the one thing you most want to do, and then spits on your sorrow over failing. Anger because you want to apologize to somebody or something, but nobody's even interested in hearing your confession. The world just sits there and says, 'Shut up. That's the way it is. You missed your chance.'

"And you know what happens then? You die. I know it sounds dramatic, but it's true. You feel utterly helpless, as if there wasn't a muscle in your body that had an ounce of life in it—as if, since you couldn't move toward that one thing, you didn't care if you never moved again."

"But that's not where you're at now, is it? You seem to have gotten past that kind of deadness somehow."

"Mostly I have; though there are times when I feel it's just walking one foot behind me, waiting to pounce on me again. Something you said helped. About God having it all straightened out, even if we can't see how it can possibly be so. I can't say I always think it will work out like that, but I try just to believe it. You get a little life back if somehow you can imagine there's another chance. It's better to believe that than to believe nothing."

She was still sitting erect, still but somehow animated. I watched her for a while before saying anything.

"I think I have at least a hint of how it works. It's mostly just a theological theory, but it's one way of talking about it. It isn't exactly that we'll be invited back into the past to take a second crack at what we didn't do well the first time. I don't think that ever happens anyway, not even when everybody is still alive and willing to stay in contact. What really happens is that, since everybody is held in Christ, no relationship is ever over. We only missed *one* chance. The obvious offering we failed to make the first time can be made in other offerings at other times. Even by other people offering for us. It's as if there wasn't just a single wire connecting you or me to Ted—in your case, the love; in mine, whatever my relationship to him was. It's more like there being a thousand wires between us and him and everybody else so that lots of things we can't see as helping him can, in Christ, be the very offerings that do the job he couldn't do."

"How do you mean?"

"Well, for instance. You were saying a minute ago that you offered up your anger. You didn't exactly *say* that, but it certainly seems as if you've *done* it. Now maybe it was true that nobody's love for Ted was strong enough to keep him from dying of his anger—maybe not even God's. But it also might be true that you're going on living after your own kind of death—your offering up of your anger—is one of the offerings that does the job of reconciliation for him. What doesn't get done one way, gets done in another. Christ just switches the wires around till he finds a live connection. That make any sense?"

"I think so. It means no one's really dead, doesn't it?"

"Exactly. But saying it like that scares the theological hell out of me, because it sounds like all the chintzy funeral-parlor poetry in the world. All I mean is that, even if I don't understand a word of it, I still choose to trust Christ when he says, 'Whoever believes in me, though he were dead, yet shall he live, and whoever lives and believes in me shall never die.' He really *is* the resurrection and the life. Not just some day, but now. And he's got it all together somehow. That's as far as I get with it, but it seems better than anything else."

"What's the point of the dying then, though? I mean, is it just sort of an unreal happening? Is it just a waste?"

"I don't think so. In Christ, the dying becomes the engine that makes the whole thing go. As a matter of fact, through Christ, death turns out to be the only engine of reconciliation there is, his death offered for all, and our deaths offered for each other. But I'm out of my depth. I came in here with an empty head. I should shut up before the vacuum inside collapses it."

"Whatever you say. But I like to hear you talk. Want something now?"

"What've you got?"

"Same as before, plus coffee or tea—and a bottle of white wine I bought since you were here."

"That sounds good. White wine."

She got up. Over to the China closet to fetch two glasses. Then to one of the end-table-cabinets. I watched her as she knelt down and got out a bottle of Widmer's Lake Niagara. She sat back on her heels, twisted halfway around toward me and held up the wine. Her breasts were silhouetted against the dark furniture.

"How's this?"

"Perfect. Just perfect."

Me, who can't stand New York State wine.

We talked for a while. She was starting Monday on a typing course, with an eye to getting enough speed back to try for some kind of office job. We rambled over the options: real estate brokers, travel agents, doctors, lawyers. I put in a plug for a lawyer's office job: Superficially, she was perfect for a travel agency but she had more on the ball than that.

There were other topics. The subject of the gossip, however, never came up, so I let it lie fallow. When it needs plowing, chances are she'll slice through it in style.

Along about three, I got up to go.

"Thanks for talking. It's nice to be able to dispense with the agenda and just ramble on. As I said, you're a good listener. And as I didn't say, you're also a good talker."

"My pleasure. It's not all that hard to talk to you. I'll probably see you Sunday. By the way, my mother is coming down tomorrow for a week. If she feels up to it, she'll be with me."

"Good. Love to meet her. Take care now."

"You too, Bill."

She stood in the doorway and waved as I pulled away.

One deep calleth to another…

All thy waves and storms are gone over me.

XXXIV

Friday, June 1st

I ENDED THE afternoon with some hospital calls and, while driving around, thought a little about tomorrow at the seminary. Since it would be the last class before the exam, and since I was really doing little more than faking out my own themes on eschatology, I decided I owed them two things: a fair warning that they were responsible for learning the old stuff on their own, and a chance to have at me on the revised imagery I was tinkering with. See if I can bail faster than they can punch holes.

When I got home, it turned out that some of the kids had gone down to the village beach at low tide and picked mussels. Liz had been planning to have pasta anyway, so I talked her into letting me make a white and a red mussel sauce.

"All right. But leave some of the plain tomato sauce plain. Not everybody is wild about mussels."

"You have anything finer than spaghetti?"

"Look in the pantry. I think there's vermicelli over on the right."

"Good. I hate eating rope."

After supper, I went into the office and threw some things into my briefcase to take to school in the morning. While clearing off the desk, I came across the note from two nights ago about calling Dick Jorjorian. Sudden notion to call him again and let him know at least that I had gone to see Anne. I dialed.

"Dick? This is Bill Jansson. I just thought I'd give you a ring and report on what I've been up to. I went to see Anne this morning."

"How was she? Was Irene right about her having added two and two?"

"Oh, she'd added them all right—and had one rotten night as a result. Took a long time to get her to the point of talking about it, but she finally did. By the time I left, she seemed a little better. I guess I'll be keeping an eye on her for a while, so let me know if you ever think of anything that might be helpful."

"I sure will. Say, Bill…"

He hesitated for several seconds.

"Yes?"

"When you talked to Anne, did you get any impression she knew more than I told you—that maybe there was other information or something she was trying to cope with?"

"No. Can't say that I did. She was upset about having

to face the identity of the mistress, but once we got past that, the conversation went pretty well. Why, though? What other information is there? There isn't another shoe left to drop, is there?"

"I don't think there's really much chance of that; but as long as you're going to keep tabs on Anne, I may as well let you in on something I didn't tell you the other day. Remember I mentioned 'a *couple* of errors?' Well, as far I know, I'm the only person who knows about the other one, but since there's no way of being sure, you might as well be prepared."

"Okay, shoot."

"Back at the beginning of April, I had to go to one of those dumb all-day conferences at the Holiday Inn in Plainview. You know, right on the Expressway where it comes close to Northern State at Sunnyside Boulevard. There's that big King's Grant Motel diagonally across from it. Anyhow, a couple of us decided after lunch to duck the panel discussion they had scheduled for two o'clock, so we wandered around outside at the edge of the parking lot.

"Well, we were yakking away, when all of a sudden, what drives in at the other end of the lot but Ted's VW with all the McGovern stickers and flower emblems. He gets out and heads for the main door. At first I thought maybe he was going into the conference, though I couldn't quite figure why the other passenger in the car didn't go in too. By and by however, he comes back out, and I get my answer. The other passenger is not a guy. When he gets near the car this…tomato gets out, and the two of them walk to the far end of the building. Up the staircase and right into the last room on the second floor."

"Didn't he see you?"

"I'm positive he didn't. He didn't look right or left—and once the guys I was talking to got a glimpse of the broad he was with, I simply turned my back to the parking lot and got all the details just by listening to cracks about how spending an afternoon with a blonde in leather boots would do more for county welfare than a month of conferences. You know. Real funny stuff unless you're in on it. I not only knew the guy. I knew the gal too."

"The blonde in leather boots? Are you kidding?"

"Absolutely not. She's a sexy kid who works somewhere in Grant Plaza. Been to church once or twice. Comes on very strong as the kind that tips over easily."

"Then it really wasn't the church school gal?"

"No way. This one is unmistakable."

"Good Lord, does that ever stir the pot! You say, though, you're the only one who knows? None of the guys you were with recognized either of them?"

"Nope. I asked."

"Nobody just faking you out, playing dumb?"

"I'm almost positive not. It was all one big joke. Besides, all those guys were from Nassau County."

"What about Irene?"

"I didn't tell her. I can keep my mouth shut too, you know. You're the only one I've told. And I'm telling you for one reason only: so you're forearmed with Anne in the unlikely case I'm wrong."

"You might well be, you know. If he'd shacked up with her other times or places, somebody else might have seen what you did."

"Maybe. But she hadn't been around long, so it couldn't have happened too often. And anyway, if there were going to be gossip about it, it would be out by now. I really don't think anybody knows a thing. As I said though, in case I'm wrong, you're a little more ready to deal with Anne than you would have been otherwise."

"Right. But good God, Richard, do you see what a bombshell you just dropped? Not just for what it might mean to Anne and the other gal—the mistress, I mean—but for what it means about Ted's death. For the first time, there seems to be a lead to what was really getting to him."

"I know that. It's been a lot to carry around by myself. I'm just glad to have another shoulder under the load, believe me."

"Any time, Richard, but I hope you don't have too many more loads to share. Anyway, if you're right, it goes no further than you and me. Let's hope for that."

"Amen. Well, listen, keep in touch. And let me know if there's anything I can do."

"I think you've done plenty for one week. I'm just going to say goodbye and try to assimilate it all. Take care, Dick. See you around."

I hung up.

God! Talk about crossed wires! Just imagine what was

going on inside Ted. What the hell was the third dame all about? Just hot pants? Tricks he hadn't tried before? Could be. Who's immune to that kind of temptation? But with Ted it would have to be converted into some big, earnest deal to take the curse off it.

And that's what caught him. If he could just have been a plain bastard he might have made it, but he had to be a sincere one. He couldn't just screw the third one; he had somehow to fall for her. And that put the double whammy on him: He zaps Anne for the second time; but worst of all, he violates once and forever the privacy of the love between himself and Pat. He was holding himself together by believing that he was good enough at least to keep his second set of books faithfully; when he found himself starting up a third, the whole jury-rigged business came unstuck.

God what a mess! Why not three sets? Even if it's wrong, why not three sets? Or five. Or a hundred? Why this self-destroying compulsion to see yourself as a good guy? Where the hell does that kind of Christian pharisaism get its justification? Why can't Ted or I or anybody just fall apart in the Everlasting Arms? Why the devilish itch to prove we can keep ourselves together and don't really need the Holding?

But the pain! The Holiday Inn. Sunnyside Boulevard and the Expressway. It's not enough for him to be a bastard; he has to make himself into a giant one. That's the motel Pat asked him to meet her at the first time—the time he insisted on going to the City instead. Crossed wires arcing all over the place in the dark. I'll bet he even had a little Chivas Regal to share with the broad. He can't just take the trick; he has to set himself up as Judas in his own mind. O Blessed Leo Durocher! Why do the nice guys *insist* on finishing last? O Saint Dorothy Parker, standing by the coffin at Scott Fitzgerald's funeral! Ted, you poor bastard. O Lamb of God, *qui tollis peccata mundi*. Why can't anyone believe he really does take away the mess? Why can't we just accept the reconciliation without going through all this vainglorious crap about how we were all right until we did the one thing that put us beyond the pale? *Libera nos Domine. Libera* Ted,

> And all poor s-o-b's who never
>   Do anything properly, spare
> Us in the youngest day…

> O, Jesus, Jesus, Jesus.

XXXV

Saturday, June 2nd

Saturday dawned clear and cool, and, as usual, I left at ten of seven for the drive in. Almost my favorite time and day. No cars on the road once you're past the marina and the launching ramp. Peaceful.

West on 25A to 347. West on 347 to Northern State. Then, in. Parkway, gold-green in the morning sun, a good thing out of Long Island after all. Thanks to Robert Moses and his talent for writing vitriolic letters and getting his own way. My father worked for him in the New York City Department of Parks during the Depression. One of a brood of out-of-work artists and delineators who took shelter under the municipality's wing and rode out some of the leanest years. Ted Kautzky was the biggest name I can remember. My father called him a great man with a pencil and raved about his work. I had a good childhood. My father was talented, and one of his talents was the ability to admire other people's work. Enthusiasm. The best gift.

Coming up on the overpass before Exit 36, I thought of Ted. Sunnyside Boulevard. By what gift do I drive by here on top of the world when he hit it at the end of his rope? Why this exit out of all of them? Was it that damned Holiday Inn just over there on the left behind those trees? Some kind of ritual propitiation? Some terrible, unnecessary immolation by a good man, while slobs like me who have it figured better cruise along untroubled by their badness? A brutal cutting off of the offending hand, while, in the mystery of the kingdom, the lecherous eye just soaks up the sunshine? Where's the equity?

Worse yet, who's to say his death doesn't smell more of Christ than my life? The kingdom of heaven suffering violence and the violent taking it by storm. God, who knows? Gooseflesh. Full eyes. Handkerchief. The puzzle of his death half-solved, but the Mystery hid deeper than ever.

Off the parkway and over to Hempstead. Pork store first: a *Rügenwälder*, Henry, and a *Hildesheimer*, a *Grober Mettwurst*, and four *Kassler Rippchen*, in one piece, *bitte. Etwas noch?* Oh, why not? *Drei Paar Landjäger—für die Kinder.* German *Wurst-names:* Music made out of pigs. Heavy stuff; but not as heavy as German theology. And not nearly as heavy as German humor: The rest of the help kid Henry; I don't catch the beginning of it, but it ends with a crack about a *yarmulke*. Anti-Semitism is alive and well in Hempstead.

Across the street to the cheese store: Feta, olives and a ripe Coulommiers for the faculty lunch table, plus a Boursault for tomorrow's cocktail hour. Seymour says how about some Halvah?

"Okay. Half a pound."

"What kind? Turkish or Greek?"

"Turkish, I guess."

"Chocolate or vanilla?"

"Vanilla."

"Plain or marbled?"

"Marbled."

"With nuts or without?"

"Decisions, decisions. With."

"You think it's easy to come in here and buy Halvah?"

Marvin adds up the column of figures, down, up, down, left to right, casting out nines in his head the way his Jewish storekeeper father taught him, and writes the sum down all at once. I'm a dollar short. Remind me next week.

Out to the car. The bag with the Jewish arithmetic on it goes next to the Karl Ehmer sack in the reconciling back seat. We shall eat and drink together in the kingdom. After a somewhat larger order of reconciliation.

XXXVI

Saturday, June 2nd

THE FIRST QUESTION thrown at me in class was from a student who had bought the idea of not using the imagery of an afterlife to figure eternal life, but who wondered where that left the resurrection of the dead.

"If you're not going to put it out at the end of time, and if you're not going to have any souls waiting around for it to happen, why can't you say that the resurrection happens at the moment of death? Your whole life has been hid with Christ in God; but it wasn't really your *whole* life until death put the last line on it. Why not say that right at death you immediately discover what he's held for you, risen glorified and reconciled?"

I said I thought that was possible, but he needed to make a distinction:

"If you're just using that as another image, it's all right. It isn't the biblical one, but let that pass. As far as I can see, it's both better and worse than the biblical one. Better, because it gets rid of all that quasi-time after death which has always made theological trouble: You don't have to fake out a purgatory for souls to pass the non-time in while waiting for the resurrection to happen, so you avoid all the waiting-room/time-in-jail imagery that threw Roman theology into a commercial system of indulgences and Protestants into a mortal terror of praying for the dead.

"But it's worse than the biblical image, because it's harder to see as real. The picture of Christ coming and raising the dead is a picture of a promise actually being fulfilled. Your picture of a person's whole life sailing into fullness at the moment of death is always going to be marred by the fact that right in the forefront of it is a very dead corpse. It looks as if an awful lot of the person didn't make the ship.

"But then you have to make still another distinction: If you're using your idea, not as an image but as a theory, that is, as a relatively straight explanation of what actually occurs, then it's no good at all. Take heart, though. The biblical picture isn't any good for that purpose either. There's just too much in the rest of the Bible about the resurrection being present and operative *right now* to allow you to confine it literally to any one moment. Since it's present in all moments, saying it happens at the end of a man's life is no improvement over saying it happens at the end of the world. Both make bad theory. Both fog up the deepest truth, which is that the resurrection, at its root in the Word of God, isn't really a happening at all. It isn't something that turns up one day, it's not a transaction by which something that wasn't so is made so; it's the eternal, non-transactional Mystery of reconciliation within the creative act of the Trinity. In this temporal world of course, it shows up as a transaction; but all through time, it's simply *present*—eternally simultaneous with every temporal event. That explain anything?"

"Yes. But why is it that resurrection in the present doesn't seem to loom as large in the Bible as resurrection in the future? If it's so central, how come most people haven't even heard of it?"

"Two reasons. The future image is a more vivid picture and upstages the other one. If I show a *Playboy* centerfold and a diagram of the Trinity, guess which one you'll remember.

"The other reason is inattention. The resurrection *as present* really does loom large in Scripture, but it has a subtle and difficult largeness, and you've got to hunt around to find where it looms. For openers, think of all the stuff in John, Ephesians, Colossians and II Corinthians about the death and resurrection of Christ being present all along: about the eternal Word coming into the world and lighting every man about the Lamb slain from the foundation of the world, about Abraham rejoicing to see Christ's day, about Jesus being the resurrection and the life right then and there in front of Lazarus' tomb, about God having already raised us up together and made us sit with Christ in heavenly places, about the Mystery, hidden from ages and generations, but now made manifest in the saints, about how, if any man be in Christ, he is a new creature, right now, because the old has passed away. Christ came precisely to raise the dead. The raising of the dead is one of the signs of the kingdom, simply because, wherever the risen King is present (even before he dies, he's the resurrection), he just has that effect on people: The hour is coming, *and now is*, when the dead shall hear the voice of the Son of God, and they that hear shall live. And then there's the Transfiguration. What's that about, if not the presence of the risen King, then and there?

"Furthermore, there's the whole sacramental system. What's Baptism? It's the effective declaration, here and now, of our full possession of the Paschal Mystery of the death and resurrection of Jesus. Same thing for the Eucharist: a showing forth of Christ's eternally present death and resurrection, day after day after day.

"When you get a little time this summer, get out Young's *Concordance* and hunt down *resurrection, risen, rise, life*, and other words like that, and chase through the passages around them: You'll see the looming fast enough. Then sandpaper your fingertips and play theological Jimmy Valentine with it all, feeling for the clicks, listening for the tumblers to fall into place. The Mystery is a well-made safe. You may not crack it, but you'll develop a healthy admiration for it. Next question."

It came from a student whose approach to theology had been through the charismatic movement, and who had a large personal investment in the literal truth of the imagery of afterlife and in the precise sequence of events at the Last Day. He was just upset at the thought of setting it aside, even for a moment.

Rule 68-A: Never approach fundamentalism head-on; cut it off from behind.

My first step was to assure him that I had no intention of doing without his favorite imagery. I only wanted to let other, equally scriptural, imagery shed its light too. But to do that, I said, you have to put the usual imagery in the shade for a while so your eyes can pick up what you're missing. Lots of stars are bigger than the sun; but you can't see them until you get the sun out of the sky for a few hours.

I then tried to get him to see that the *Last* Day was only one of many biblical uses of a major image. The word *day* should be hunted down in the concordance, too, and the different uses of it allowed to interpenetrate each other. I wasn't suggesting he go back on Scripture; I was urging him to go back *to* Scripture and let it comment on itself.

I threw him a sampling: the judgment-laden *day of the Lord* from the Old Testament; Christ's *at that day* and *in that day*; Abraham, four hundred and thirty years before Moses, rejoicing to see *Christ's day*. I reminded him of the days which would come when we would desire to see one of the *days* of the Lord, and of the kingdom within, that cometh not by observation because *now* is the *day* of Salvation. I took off from there into those parallels of day:

time and *hour*; the *time* as fulfilled at the very beginning of Jesus' preaching; Jerusalem, wept over by Christ because she knew not the *time* of her visitation; and above all, in John's Gospel, the *hour* which is coming and now is. Then I shifted to the *daysman* Job longed for, and the *dayspring from on high* who is Christ. Which, I pointed out, is the morning star, and gets you to the word *light*—and still another go-around with the concordance.

Someone said that was mind-blowing. I agreed, but refined the image: not blowing, as in blowing a fuse or blowing out a candle, but blowing, as in blowing up a balloon—expanding, filling, inbreathing, inspiring. There were ladies present, so I omitted the obvious, pleasurable extension of the imagery, and called for the next question. It came from one of my best scholastic logic-choppers:

"Back at the beginning of the course, you said that things exist *properly*—as themselves, in their own proper being—only in themselves; and that when you talk about the way they exist in God, you have to say they exist in him only causatively, or exemplarily, or eminently. Now. In your theology, the final order—heaven, or the reconciled state, or the New Jerusalem, or whatever—exists only in God. You're saying that our eternal life is simply the life we had here, held in God for everlasting exploration. But. Doesn't that mean that we have no *proper* eternal existence—that we exist forever only as one of God's thoughts and not in our own right?"

I thought that one over for a minute and then went after it.

"Well, at least somebody reads the notes. You have to remember, though, that my notes are not always backed up by Aquinas, or even by me. Some of them are unreconstructed scholastic theology manual stuff. For a corrective, you ought to read Owen Barfield's *Saving the Appearances:* He's very strong on St. Thomas; but you'll find he gives a better view of what you're saying than manual theology does.

"I think the answer to your question is, that the distinction between exemplary and proper existence is helpful only when you're talking about God as God. It was devised to keep you from smudging up the divine being with material attributes—to preclude your saying things like: Since God causes apple pies by an eternal act of his divine mind, the divine mind is a boxful of apple pies. In other words, it's designed to guard against pantheism, or emanationism, or something. It should be used only to protect the proper existence of God, not to denigrate the proper, eternal existence of creatures.

"Barfield finds the way out of the difficulty in the Thomistic notion of *participation:* We aren't, even now, just utterly separate from the divine mind: We *participate* in the divine being by our very nature. Analogically, of course; but by an analogy of being, not just a purely mental one. Look it up.

"My own way of handling it would be a little different. I would suggest that you're underestimating what it means to exist only as one of God's thoughts. I would say that even in our present existence—with all its convincingly real, earthy solidity—we can also be said to exist only as one of God's thoughts. The trick is, you have to get that sleeper of an 'only' out of there. Why say only? What's so 'only' about the creative intelligence of God? His thoughts have hair on them. His creating Word has a bark to it. Whatever Jahweh *thinks*, Jahweh gets.

"If you want to protect the reality, the propriety of eternal human existence, don't go with the exemplary/proper distinction. Start by saying that we exist properly in two styles. To use Barfield's terminology: We exist in the style of *original participation*, and in the style of *final participation*. *Original*, being roughly the way we exist *in the body*, and *final*, the more open, full way we exist *in Christ*. Both styles coexist right now. The history of salvation is really the history of the unveiling of the second within the first. But again, read Barfield and let me know what you think.

"One more thought, though. About the styles of participation. Why two? Maybe the answer is that just for the fun of it, God likes more than one style in his mind at once. Maybe he's just a virtuoso whistler, and whistles the song of creation in double stops, for the pure pleasure of doing so. What we hear now is mostly only the bass line, the original participation—with every now and then a hint of the melody, the final participation. Or maybe he's the eternal Isaac Stern, and is fiddling us into being in triple stops. Maybe, in the opening out of the web, he does it in 'n' stops, in an infinite number of styles of participation. Why not?

"But in any case, the virtue of saying it my way is that every one of the two, three, or 'n' styles of participative being is *really, properly*, existent as itself, and not just as a purely divine notion. All of them—in the flesh or in Christ, in the body or with the Lord—are real existences in the Land of the Trinity, the only homeland we've ever had, the real *there* we've always been, the final *place*, where, in perichoresis, the Word and the Spirit have forever offered us, along with the beer, and the pretzels, and the pumpernickel and the *wurst*, into the exchanges of the Father's picnic.

"Yummy stuff, *nicht wahr? Wurstgeschäfliche Theologie.*"

XXXVII

Saturday, June 2nd

There were two or three more questions, but eventually it was time to break for mass and lunch.

At the table, the conversation turned to the subject of a priest who'd recently resigned his parish after a couple of years of typical, stupid infighting. I had gone to fetch the Vermouth and when I got back, Jim Bates was asking Ed Lawrence,

"What on earth was all the fuss about?"

"Actually, nothing much. The parish had bad habits from his predecessor's pussyfooting incumbency. They were used to jumping all over him, telling him what he could and couldn't do, and complaining about it all either way. Harry started out trying to hold the line, but they finally found his weak spot and got to him. The situation was really not much more than a matter of divergent styles, but the combination of sick parish and sincere priest enabled them to pick at him. You know. Why hadn't he seen Mrs. so-and-so in the hospital? Why was he always late for meetings? Why wasn't he out making parish calls? Why had he offended Mr. X? Crap like that. It's the old ploy: If you can't catch him in bed with somebody, get him to convince himself he's a lousy priest—on your terms of course—and he'll take himself out of the game for you. Bastards!"

Guy Ferretti spit an olive pit neatly into the ashtray.

"We ought to give a course here in power politics. We teach them what the meat and potatoes of theology taste like, but then when they get out in the church, it makes them so sick to their stomach they can't stand the sight of food. Let's see. Why don't we call the course, 'Wheeling and Dealing 101, or, How to be a bigger bastard than they are.'"

Art Hellweg suggested a different title: "Priestcraft and karate: the pastoral hand as deadly weapon."

Turner Adams, who had dropped in for his free noon drink in the middle of Ed's remarks, spoke up.

"You're on the right track, but you've got to have me in for a guest lecture. I've got one on 'The parish priest as steel-centered marshmallow.' The hard-nosed approach makes unnecessary enemies. It's only the ones who try to bite you in two you have to worry about, so you get very clear about what you won't budge on, and you graciously give in on all the rest. That way, most people find you nice and sweet, but when the nasties sink their teeth into you, they break their jaws on the ball-bearing in the middle.

My subtitle is: 'How to say, So far and no further, and make them know you mean it.'"

Jim got serious.

"It's not all that easy, though. Some people just aren't political enough to survive. It's all right for you politicians to sit around and give out free advice, but when a non-political type gets into some parochial whirlpool, he needs more than advice. He needs present help. I keep going back to what I said at Ted Jacobs's funeral. I still don't know what his death was all about, but at least it's a rebuke to our whole system of mutual non-support. In the Episcopal Church the two most likely helps to a priest in trouble are mostly absent, or worse: His brother priests are off in their little successpools sipping Vermouth; and the Bishops, half the time, end up playing footsie with the laity."

I agreed:

"That's right. And the successes we console ourselves with aren't all that hot, either. Next year's budget still hasn't been approved, you know. Sometimes I think all we've really done is taken a couple of leaks in the corridors of power."

XXXVIII

Sunday, June 3rd

On Sunday morning, I got up at three-thirty, made some sermon notes, read a short story in the *New Yorker* and went back to bed. My feet were cold. Long, half-wakeful time waiting for them to warm.

I am walking west on the grass along Northern State Parkway, approaching Exit 36. Straight, steady rain falling. No traffic at all. As I come around the bend, I see Ted's car, still smoking, smashed into the abutment of the overpass. Odd feeling: no surprise, no horror, no particular curiosity, no breaking into a run to get to it. I walk to the car in the time it takes, and look in. He is obviously dead: engine half-way into the front seat; steering wheel, dashboard, seatback, Ted—all compressed into the space of a foot, front to back. Ted's face is not visible, just the left-hand edge of his beard. I walk up to the abutment.

One of the facing-stones is cracked from the impact

of the crash; I run my finger along the crevice. Slight tremor in the rock. The crack widens a little and the wind springs up behind me, driving the rain, and plastering my shirt to my back. I shiver. The crack widens and lengthens. The wind increases. Not so much blowing toward the crack as being sucked into it. I start to step back, away from what is now a high, narrow cave-opening, but too late: I am pulled, with a tremendous burst of speed, into a short tunnel which goes straight ahead, dead level, toward a patch of blue sky. The end opens out into a field of wild flowers and low bushes. One tree in the middle, about fifty yards away.

The wind drops abruptly. I look back through the tunnel: The car is there, still smoking; the outline of Ted's beard is still visible. Strange impression, though: I feel that, somehow, he went into the tunnel just before me. All of him, too; not just his soul, but his body as well. But what is left at the other end, in the wreck, is also all of Ted. And yet, no impression of his being two: He is just there and here, too. Drumbeat, singsong chant in my head: Too, not two; Too, not two.

I turn around and walk toward the tree. It is an old oak, mostly dead and broken-branched, but spring-green in a few places. Huge trunk, four-and-a-half, maybe five feet across. Funny, weathered three-storied birdhouse about twenty feet up. Cheap Barclay Street plaster crucifix set at eye level, facing the tunnel across the field. Religious *shlock*, except for one oddity: The inscription over the head of the corpus is not the usual INRI. It reads—in

EXIT 36

Hebrew, Greek and Latin—

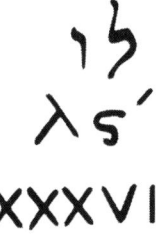

XXXVI

I walk around the tree to the other side. Audrey is sitting with her back against the trunk, chewing on a piece of grass. She is wearing faded jeans, old sneakers, and a long magenta brocaded silk tunic. Her hair is down. I'm not surprised, really; but for the first time, I'm curious:

"What are you doing here?"

"Oh, hi. I'm on duty today. What are you doing here?"

"Beats me. What do you mean, duty?"

"Every now and then I have to cover for one of them. It doesn't happen too often, so it's not really an inconvenience. As a matter of fact, it's almost always at night. Bill sleeps as if he were dead, so it doesn't bother him, and I've got nothing better to do."

"Them? Who's them?"

"The *Lamed-vovniks*."

"You mean like in the *Last of the Just*? The thirty-six unknown guys who are always in the world, keeping away the wrath of God?"

"That's more or less right. Except it's not just guys."

I think to myself, Holy smoke, all these years I've

known her, and I never even suspected. I still can't make sense of it, though.

"Are you one of them?"

"They have a policy about not telling you, so I don't know. I've never seen all thirty-six of them at once. The most I've ever seen together were about twenty. They had a meeting at this tree and they let me sit in, so I guess I might be one. But I'm not really sure. All the rest I've met are men. For all I know, it could be a sexist outfit. I am covering, though. So at least they're not chauvinistic about it."

"What do you do when you 'cover'?"

"Just talk to anybody who comes through the tunnel. Tell them how to get different places, if they want to know."

"Boy, that's weird. How do you get here, through the tunnel?"

"No. The tunnel is for the clients. I get here another way. I don't quite understand it myself, but they have a way of getting me when they want me."

"You been here long?"

"Hard to tell. When I get back home, it doesn't seem much later than when I left. But you know me and time. All my clocks are different, so I never bother to check it out."

"Hey, listen. These clients. Why do they come here?"

"Because they've died, of course."

"That's what I was afraid of. Does that mean I'm dead?"

"You have to make a distinction. First of all, if you're out here in the field, you're not dead. They have a rule: There's only one place where you can use the word 'dead,' and that's in the tunnel. They insist you say 'died' for anybody who comes through. You can use 'dead' for people on the other side of the tunnel, though. Were you dead on the other side?"

"Not as far as I know. At least I didn't feel anything I was just walking in the rain, and I came up to this wrecked car next to an overpass on Northern State. It was a friend of mine. It looked as if it just happened. Well, anyway, I was looking at this crack in the stone and I got sucked right through into here."

"Oh, one of those. I'm not an authority, of course, but my guess would be you haven't died. You'll find out easily enough: If you can walk back out the tunnel you're still alive; if you can't, you're dead. Unless you come back out this way. Then you're alive. It sounds complicated, but it's really simple."

"Wild. Absolutely wild. Say, have you seen my friend?"

"Not since I've been on duty. You're the only one that's come along. Was he really dead on the other side?"

"Oh my, yes. It was a ghastly wreck. All scrunched up. He must've been going eighty when he hit the bridge."

"Well, if he was really dead, and if he hasn't come out here, he's still in the tunnel."

I think for a little. Something isn't right.

"Why hasn't he come out?"

"I don't know. I never came through the tunnel. And

once anybody else gets out here, they don't remember a thing about it."

"Hey, Audrey. I've got an idea. When I go back into the tunnel, if he's there and he's really died, I'll send him out to you. You'll really like him. But if he hasn't died, and if I haven't either, I'll take him back out with me."

"As far as I know, that won't work. Did you see him on your way in?"

"No. It all happened too fast."

"Figures. Nobody on this side ever sees anybody in that tunnel. There are supposed to be millions in there, though. At least, that's what most of them say. There's one very old man who swears there are none, but he can't prove it, so the rest don't listen to him. My theory is that either he's right, or the dead ones in there are so invisible and thin you couldn't find them if you tried. When you go back in, though, if you find you can't go through, come back out this way. Be sure you do. Please. I want to see you again."

"What happens, if I do that? I mean, what do you do with me?"

"I give you this tunic I've got on."

"What do you wear in its place?"

"Nothing. As soon as I give it away, I go off duty. Somebody else comes and covers for me."

XXXIX

Sunday, June 3rd

Liz's coughing woke me. She got up and hunted for some cough syrup; I fished under the pillow for my watch: 5:05. Too early to get up. Anyway, I wanted to go back to the same dream and ask Audrey some more questions. Not that I'd ever been able to do that. Still, I hoped I could. Liz got back in bed.

"You been up already?"

"Sure, three-thirty. Want to get up early?"

"What time are you going out running?"

"Six, I guess."

"Call me then. Night night."

"Night."

My feet were still cold. I lay on my back and repeated my version of the Jesus prayer to the rhythm of my breathing:

Jesus, Jesus, Jesus,
Jesus, Jesus, Jesus,
Jesus, Jesus, Jesus, Jesus,
I love you, I love you, I love you.

Jesus, Jesus, Jesus,
Jesus, Jesus, Jesus,
Jesus…

I AM IN the sacristy of the church, starting to vest for the ten-thirty mass. I put on the amice, alb and cincture the altar guild has laid out on the vesting table, and open the drawer with the green vestments in it. No chasuble, no stole. I remember now that I left them in the car after saying mass at the nursing home on Friday. Out to get them, via the narrow passageway behind the altar.

Peter comes toward me.

"Father? Do you have a minute? I fixed all the kneelers except the one in the first pew on the left-hand side. Would you mind if I closed that off? It's not safe until I make a new wall fitting. Someone will surely drop it on his foot."

"Okay, Peter. Whatever you say. Thanks."

The back room at the other end of the passageway is full of people. Some kind of coffeeless coffee hour in progress. Everybody well dressed; men in light suits, women in summery dresses. Lots of wide-brimmed floppy hats; white, yellow, pale blue. Pretty.

I start to head out the back door to the parking lot,

but just as I get to it, Turner Adams, vested exactly as I am, but with a stole, comes up the steps and pushes me back in.

"How are you this morning. William me boy?"

"Adams! What are you doing here?"

"I have a little business to do with you, and it's such a beautiful morning, I thought I'd treat myself to a nice, quiet drive out here."

"You have business? With me? What business?"

"Come into the church."

"The sacristy's empty. Let's go there."

"No, the church. I want you to see something. Then we can go out front and talk on the lawn."

"Adams! I have to say mass in about thirty seconds and my vestments are out in the car. Later, all right?"

"No. Now. Come on."

We work our way through the crowd over to the door that opens into the church by the organ. On the way, Adams says,

"The Cardinal says he's sorry, but it was simply out of the question. Other plans."

"What are you talking about? What Cardinal?"

"Richard Cushing. He said you filed a petition requesting that Ted Jacobs's wife wouldn't move into your parish. Something about conflict of interest, I gather. Anyway, he passed it along, but it got turned down."

I went into the church first.

"What do you mean, turned down?"

"In about six weeks, she's going to buy in Mt. Sinai.

Nice little place."

"How do you know all this? When I saw her, she didn't say anything about moving."

"She didn't know when she saw you. She put a binder on the house just yesterday. Look in the next-to-the-last pew on the gospel side."

Sure enough, Anne Jacobs. Three rows behind Pat Donahue. Across from Liz, who is four rows behind Audrey. Great.

"Adams, what are you up to?"

"Come, come, William. You've been in the church long enough to know it's not me. It's *them*. Let's go outside."

"But I've got to say mass. I'm late already. This is ridiculous."

He took me by the arm and walked me down the aisle. Out onto the steps. The street in front of the church was gone. In its place was a kind of park, about five hundred yards long and a hundred yards wide. Tall trees at the far ends. In the center a large, oblong sunken lawn, privet-bordered, with a fountain in the middle. At the opposite side, a row of houses, all elegant, old, shingle-and-clapboard mansions, the one on the far right being Audrey's. Not obviously Audrey's. It was twice as big, had porches on three sides, and a great, sloping lawn. Still though, somehow, definitely Audrey's.

"William, forget about mass for a while. Come sit by the fountain while I fill you in."

We went across the lawn and sat on a marble bench.

EXIT 36

Bright sunlight, deep greens; more summery-looking people strolling on the grass, dresses rippling in the light breeze.

"Okay now, Adams. Just what are you—or they—up to? Who are they? Are you in on this Thirty-Six Just Men business—this *Lamed-vovnik* stuff?"

"Oh, you know about that. I suppose I should have expected; but they play their cards so close to the tunic, you get out of the habit of trying to second-guess them."

"Don't tell me you're one of them, too."

"You never know. I've never seen—"

"Hey, Adams. This is weird. I had this same conversation with a parishioner of mine in a dream last night. The rest of the line is '…more than twenty of them together at once,' right?"

"Almost. Except I've never seen more than five. What's the name of this parishioner who saw twenty?"

"Audrey."

"Oh, that one. I've met her. She's supposed to be one of the big wheels. Comes on the job in blue jeans and sneakers, right? Good-looking, late forties, long hair? She strikes me as a pretty offhand piece of work, but they must know what they're doing. What was your meeting with her all about? I mean, where did you meet her?"

"Under a tree, in a big field. It had a crucifix with the inscription replaced by the number 36 in Hebrew, Greek and Latin. I got there through this weird tunnel in a rock."

"You got there through the tunnel?"

"What do you mean *the* tunnel? I was just standing

next to Ted Jacobs's wrecked car, fingering a crack in one of the stones on the bridge, and all of a sudden, I got sucked through into the field."

"Holy cow! You actually went through it? How'd you get back out?"

"I don't know, Adams. It was just a dream. My wife had a coughing fit and woke me up before that part had a chance to happen."

"Well, William, old buddy, all I can say is you're getting special treatment. Nobody I know has ever gone in that way. What was it like?"

"Nothing much. Just in and right out. Like the wind. Audrey said something about there being lots of people kind of stuck in there. A lot of stuff about their being dead as long as they were in there. But I didn't see anybody."

Adams scratched his head and started weaving the end of his cincture through the fingers of his left hand.

"Still though, they must've let you do that for a reason. Something to do with Ted, maybe?"

"That's possible. I remember thinking he had gone in just ahead of me; but when I asked Audrey about him, she hadn't seen him. You think maybe he came out before she went on duty?"

"Maybe. But not likely. The reason I'm here is to tell you they want you to work on him and his wife and his girl friend so they don't do something stupid and decide to stay in the tunnel."

"The wife and the girl friend I've got, I guess. But

what am I supposed to do about Ted? I thought the saints in heaven were the ones who took care of cases like his. Why do they want to give the job to jokers like you and me?"

"Beats me, Billy. Maybe the saints just forget all about the tunnel, so the job of getting people out has to be done by us because we still have it in mind. But who knows? I just do what I'm told. No questions asked."

"Holy smoke, though. That tunnel has got to be the Second Death, or something. Is it really possible for anybody to come out of it after they've stayed in?"

"I don't know, kiddo. You're the theologian. My trade is scratching Bishops' backs and shuffling paper. You saw the tunnel. Has it got bars or doors on it?"

"No. Wide open at both ends."

"Well, then, it doesn't look as if anybody's *forcing* him to stay in there, does it?"

"No, I guess not."

"So work on talking him out of there. He seems to be the only problem."

"But how, Adams? How do you talk somebody into going through to the other side, when you're not even in touch with him?"

"You're not supposed to say 'other side.' The rule says you have to side 'inside'—something to do with Christ's death and resurrection being inside you already. But you know me. Theology always puts me to sleep. I just do what I'm told."

"Okay. But still, how? What do you do?"

"Well, they taught me a couple of tricks. You know, at mass, after the consecration, there's the silence, and then you break the host and throw a piece in the chalice? They claim that's a good place for pleading with somebody to go inside. It's quiet and, if the church isn't very well lit, the wine in the chalice looks real black, and you think of Christ's death, and everybody else's death inside that, and you just pray that all the sins will sink down into the dark and all the people will wise up and go on through into his resurrection. Simple, huh?"

"Terrific. What else did they tell you?"

"Oh, they've got lots of gimmicks. There's his thing they do whenever they hear that somebody—"

The alarm went off and I staggered over to the bureau. Disoriented, I knocked the clock onto the floor and under the bed.

It ran down by itself before I found it.

XL

Sunday, June 3rd

It was five-forty-five. I put on old clothes and sneakers, woke Liz and went out for a run.

Up East Broadway and north to the golf course. Sun up. Heavy dew. East across the golf course and down to Mt. Sinai harbor. Around the beach to Crystal Brook. Two and a half miles. Rest.

Shady spot on the wooded hillside facing the flats. Low tide. Stretch out on the ground and look out at the sky between the treetops. Or look *in* at the sky? Who knows?

Some gulls keening in the distance. Whistling buoy every fifteen seconds out in the sound. Two crows flying due south across Crystal Brook, cawing like a couple of businessmen following each other down a corridor, discussing what they'll say to old so-and-so in the office at the end. Two ducks, taking off in a whirr and backwinding down with a splash, fifty feet away. Wood doves far off: *Poo-whoo-oot. Poot. Poot. Poot.* Peaceful. My hands and face steam in the morning dampness.

Up again and running. Through Crystal Brook Hollow, up Old Post Road, past Audrey's. She's in the backyard, taking out the trash.

"Morning, Madam. The Lady from Proverbs 31 strikes again. You're up early."

"I woke up and couldn't go back to sleep, so I decided to cleanse the stables. You're steaming like an old horse."

"Purifies the system."

"That's a big project."

"None of your lip this morning, Love. I know something you don't know."

"Don't be so sure. I'll see you in church."

ABOUT THE AUTHOR

Robert Farrar Capon was an Episcopal priest, writer, and chef who authored many books during his lifetime, all of which insisted on good humor, good food, and the mercy of God. He lived with his wife, Valerie, on Shelter Island in NY, until he passed away in 2013.

ACKNOWLEDGEMENTS

For the publication of this book, we are indebted first and foremost to Robert's wife, Valerie Capon, who so generously chose us to help resurrect his work and who has provided invaluable and insightful guidance throughout the process. Thank you to the Rt. Rev. C. Andrew Doyle and the Episcopal Diocese of Texas, and to the Rt. Rev. Scott Benhase and the Episcopal Diocese of Georgia, for their support of Mockingbird and especially of this project; to the Rev. Mark Strobel, Laura Bondarchuk, Maddy Green, Margaret Pope, Jeff Dillenbeck, Kendall Gunter, and CJ Green; to all of our readers, donors, and supporters—thank you.

ABOUT MOCKINGBIRD

Founded in 2007, Mockingbird is an organization devoted to connecting the Christian faith with the realities of everyday life in fresh and down-to-earth ways. We do this primarily, but not exclusively, through our publications, conferences, and online resources. To find out more, visit us at mbird.com or e-mail us at info@mbird.com.